Anna A. Wright

More Truth Than Poetry

Anna A. Wright

More Truth Than Poetry

ISBN/EAN: 9783337118730

Printed in Europe, USA, Canada, Australia, Japan

Cover: Foto ©Andreas Hilbeck / pixelio.de

More available books at **www.hansebooks.com**

MORE TRUTH

THAN

POETRY

By ANNA A. WRIGHT.

1884.

CONTENTS.

CONTENTS.

ILLUSTRATIONS.

~⊙⅋⊙~

INTRODUCTION.

HAVE been induced to offer the contents
of this book to the public by the earnest
solicitations of many friends, and thus I
comply, without apologising or making re-
marks concerning the pieces; suffice to say,
two months ago the thought of writing the
same was far from me. I will ask critics to
consider several things;

First:—Kansas does not boast, as yet, of
her literary talent.

Second:—The composer and writer is a
Kansan.

Third:—She was married very young,
went into a family of considerable size; con-
sequently the cares of a family and numer-

ous household duties absorbed all working hours, leaving the writer with little or no time for study. But, as work cannot chain the intellectual part, we are at liberty to look back through departed years, and note the great and wonderful changes that have taken place since the soil of this fair domain ceased to be trampled by British oppressors.

The heart of every true American must glow with rapturous delight when contemplating the advantages and progress of our country, knowing there is no higher title, no more honored name, than they possess, —American citizens! We can look back through the short period of forty years, and see that immense concourse of American people assembled around the completed monument of Bunker Hill, upon the soil which will be ever dear to the bosom of the patriot, and to the friends of liberty throughout the world. That vast multitude listened with intense interest to America's greatest orator, while he poured forth, in words of unparalleled eloquence, his love and devotion to his country and his countrymen;

while each heart beat in quick response to the patriotic exultation, ''thank God, I, also, am an American!'' If America to-day could boast of more sons possessed with such unalloyed and profound patriotism, there would be less wrangling among politicians.

In contemplating America's wonderful progress, we will notice, in particular, our beloved State of Kansas. For what interests the people of Kansas, must materially interest the people of every other state in the Union. As Kansas is a representative of every state, and as Kansas in particular is on trial before the nation, she is to demonstrate how strong is her ideal of a practical manhood, that has enough austere virtue and manly love for the will of the people, to declare that the mandates of courts, and the solemn sanction of the organic act must and shall be enforced.

To the perpetual shame of Kansas—this grand and noble young state, to which many have given a quarter of a century of unbroken love and devotion — we shrink to say there is witnessed the dance of death,

INTRODUCTION.

and disgraceful orgies of violated laws; death to the principle that makes popular liberty possible! and for which Kansas suffered and sacrificed so much in her grandly heroic days. Is it possible that upon the soil where Kansas martyrs shed their blood for liberty and the upholding of her laws; where her true and law-abiding citizens were hunted and hounded in repelling ruffianly violators of the law; there is to be a brazen and bawdy prostitution of a law and its wanton violation flouted in the faces of the people, whose representatives, by a vote practically unanimous, enacted? The noes come from woodland and prairie. From the waters of the Blue and Vermillion, in the north; from the sandy plains in the west; from the banks of the Neosho and Arkansas; there comes one voice, "the law of Temperance must be enforced." From every grove and valley that is familiar with the story of what Kansas martyrs suffered and dared twenty-five years ago, for the right and) to uphold the supremacy and majesty of violated law), there should go up one voice, "the law of Temperance must be enforced." Because it is the law, and because it is right. The protests of the people ought to go up so strong and united that the cowards would flee to the dessert, rather than witness the desecration of law. The violators should be made to feel and know that they are making themselves infamous, and scandalizing the brightest and best portion of the history of the grandest state in the Union. No interest of Kansas has been injured by the adoption of the Prohibition amendment. It has not stopped immigration. Building has not ceased, but has increased ten-fold. Kansas skies are just as bright and inviting as ever. The climate and bountiful crops which woo and win the industrious settler, appear more genial and bountiful than ever before in the years of phenominal and wonderful growth. In this prosperous young state, farms are being opened up every day; the future of Kansas was never so bright, never painted with such gorgeous colors of golden promise to the heroic, the grand and glorious

State of Kansas, as since the adoption of
the Prohibition amendment. Kansas will
never suffer for doing right. When wheat
mills take the place of whisky mills, and
corn is grown where whisky has raised
weeds and thistles; the wife and children
have the proceeds, instead of the saloon-
keeper; manufactories take the place of gin
shops; then the community will walk upright, and the country be on the road to
prosperity.

We can look back through less than one-
third of a century and see the wild, unbroken
prairies for hundreds of miles in either direction, with scarcely a vistage of civilization;
there was nothing that human hands had
done to develop nature from her primeval
solitudes. The waters of the Blue, Kansas,
and their tributaries in the north and east;
the numerous small streams that form the
Solomon in the more central part; the
Neosho and its branches in the east; the
Arkansas, and the multitude of creeks that
flow into it in the south and west; all
flowed on uninterrupted, as they had done

for centuries. The melody of the birds, the countless herds of buffalo, the antelope, elk, deer and small animals, were undisturbed by the voice of human industry. Spread out as far as the eye could reach in either direction was an endless carpet of verdure and beauty. Broad prairies, covered with rich coating of luxuriant grass; beautiful parks, formed by nature, but seemingly adorned by art, lined the gently sloping hillsides; rich valleys and beautiful uplands, awaited the plow and hoe of the husbandman, that they might laugh with abundant harvest. Here was beauty without productiveness. Utility had not changed nature to the care of progress, and compelled her to contribute to the comforts, the luxuries and the happiness of mankind.

The same heavens are still over us, the same sun sheds its effulgent rays upon our soil. The same streams murmur their musical sounds and pass on unvexed to the sun-lit sea. But all else, how changed! Waving fields of grain; the silver tasseled corn; all kinds of cereals; beautiful groves and orchards bearing all kinds of fruit in their season; substantial stone, brick and frame buildings; stone hedge, board and wire fences, have taken the place of the wild, unbroken prairie, the dug-out, straw stable and lariat.

THE AUTHOR.

Barnes, Kansas, 1884.

PART I.
KANSAS.

Kansas Struggling for a Foothold.

EXPLORERS, hunters and miners,
    Had crossed those lovely plains,
When naught but the savage Indian
    Held sway o'er these domains.

But the onward words of America's son's
    Were, "westward we will go!
And on those rich and verdant plains,
    We'll wield the plow and hoe!"

At first her growth was very slow.
    But healthy it must be;
For free-soil men couldn't go a law
    Called "Squatter Sovereignty."

In '58 another dose was mixed—
    And it was a bitter pill!—
It was got up by a dough-faced son,
    And known as the "English Bill."

For thirty years they've made their home
    Upon the Kansas soil;
But grasshoppers, drouths and prairie fires
    Have made them double toil.

But now, such things she looks upon
    As a relic of the past;
For in her mighty strides to win,
    Some states she's sweeping past.

In '59 they tried to get
    The first pre-emption through;
But the blue lodge clan, who lived in the south
    Said, "Boys 'twill never do!"

Next they tried for a homestead bill,
    And they thought they'd get it;
It passed the house—Republican,—
    But 'twas defeated in the senate.

Election in Atchison, Kansas, in 1858

Again the bill was read and referred,
  With many a hot discussion, too;
But the solid south and dough-faced north
  Said, "Boys it shan't go through!"

And then the issue came, you know,
  The south against the north;
Again they thought they'd try the bill,
  To see what 'twould bring forth.

Just then a gale from the south swept by.
  It said, "we're all prepared for war!
Resign your seats and come at once,
  For free-soil men we do abhor!"

And when the pests had left the house,
  They who had tried to crush this state
With insults, more than men could bear,
  With loud harangue and mean debate,

The free-soil men watched the gale,
  To see what it would waft,
When English said, "I'll vote it now,

For Jimmy B—— will veto that,
He'll crush it afore and aft!"

For six long years of Democratic rule
'Twas broils, blood-shed and strife;
For ruffiains, from the border states,
Marched through with lead and knife.

She had no power such mobs to stay,
For trampled had been her laws
By the very men who had said,
Our constitution and our laws,
They would sustain to the last clause.

And thus, you see, they bound her down,
Till eighteen sixty-one,—
Old Abe took the reins, you know,—
And then, she walked alone.

And through that long and bloody strife,
She filled her quota full;
And since that time she's rushed ahead
Each year, and made some giant strides,
While under Republican rule.

She had the best of Governors, too,
    From Robison to St. John;
They were just the men to hold the reign,
    And drive her right along.

Thus Kansas, in her younger days,
    Was like a tender sprout;
She was nipped and stunted by the men
Who now, for a blind, with swelling words,
    Cry, "turn the rascals out!" ·

The Kansas Boy.

SEE the merry Kansas boy,
   Rise at dawn of day,—
Do his chores, and eat his hash,
   And then to the field away.

Then turn the furrows, one by one,
   Till he hears the well-known ring
Of the dear old bell by the kitchen door,
   When his mother pulls the string.

And then with a smile and a quickened step,
   The traces he will drop;
Fold up the lines, and away they'll go,
   Till by the well they'll stop.

And when he's eaten a good square meal,
And the hour for rest is done,
He'll turn the furrows as before,
Till the setting of the sun.

Thus, day by day, his work's the same,
Till the plowing is all through;
And then he'll sow and plant his grain,—
For that's the way they do.

And then it's harrow day by day,
Then roll the same ground o'er,
Until it looks like a garden bed,
And smooth as a kitchen floor.

And then there comes the steady tramp,
To cultivate the corn,
Until the golden fields of grain
Say, "boy, I must be shorn."

Then it's reap and shock the grain,
And make the giant stacks;
Which make the boys so tired at night,
And many aching backs.

Then of his grass, so fine and sweet
   He mows a goodly store;
Then stacks it up for winter use,
   An hundred ton or more.

And then it's thresh and plow again,
   And sow the garnered wheat;
And that's the way the Kansas boy
   Gets up the bread you eat.

He gathers in his pumpkins,—
   His potatoes are so fine,—
He gathers in his apples,
   And clusters from the vine.

And then a tiresome job begins,
   When the silvered corn is ripe;
It's husk and crib and do his chores.
   And work with all his might.

His work is hard in summer,
   But winter brings repose,
When he takes his hat and books you know
   And off to school he goes.

And there he'll sit on a patent seat,
  And con his lessons o'er,
Unmindful of the log school house,
  Where his father gained his lore.

He'll see before him on a map,
  A spot all dotted o'er
With cities, towns and villages,
  Full twenty score or more.

That spot was then a treeless plain,
  Far from the homes of cultured men
In the olden days when they whipped by rule
  And sat on a slab in the district school.

He thinks the wise would have laughed in
    scorn,
  Had men foretold our fields of corn;
Ah! they knew not the wealth untold
  That was hid where the Kansas Prairies
    rolled.

He never walks, but always rides,
  If it's only half a mile,

He'll mount the fleetest horse in the barn,
　For that's the Kansas style.

He's not the boy of which you sing,
　That borrows of his dad,
But holds the rein above his own,
　Of the best that can be had.

His steers and hogs are fattened
　On the corn his hands did raise,
And then he takes them off to town,
　For thus he thinks it pays.

Success attends the Kansas Boy,
　Who merrily follows his plow;
He's monarch of Prairie and upland;--
　'Tis only to God he must bow.

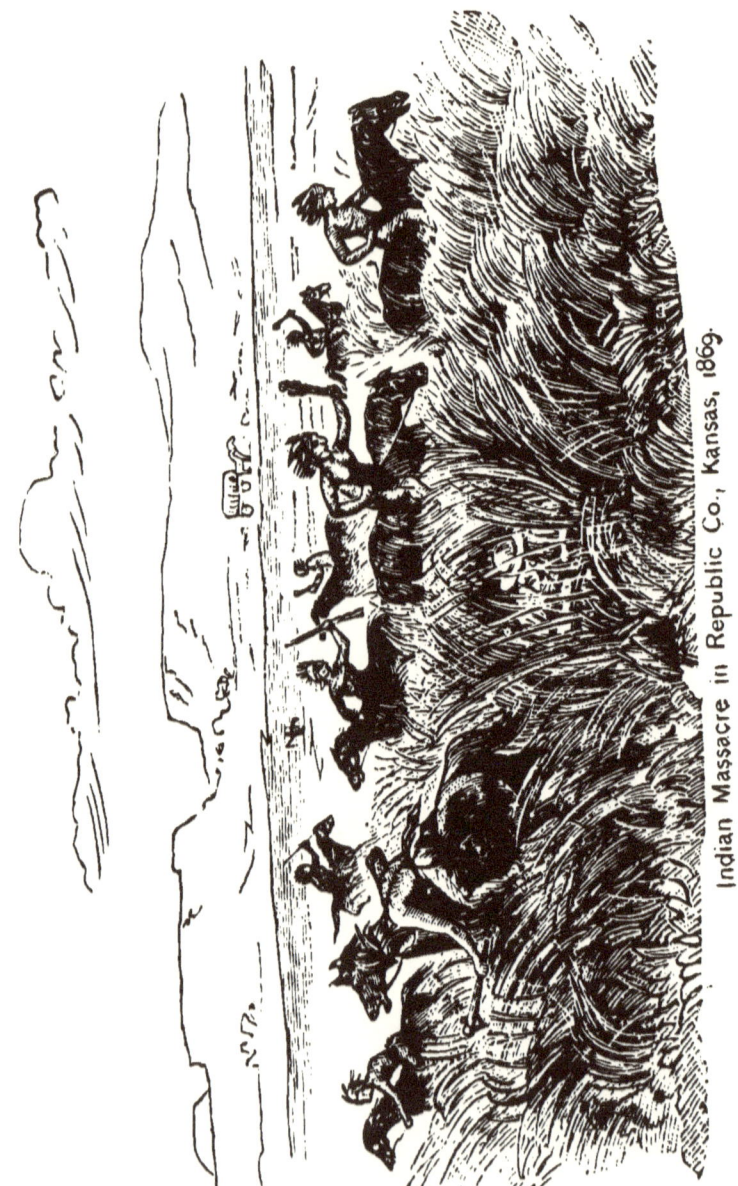

Indian Massacre in Republic Co., Kansas, 1869.

Sketch of the Buffalo and Indian Massacre.

———•◦◦✖◦◦•———

T the period when immigrants began to make settlements along the frontier of Kansas, buffalo was found in the eastern part of the state, but they gradually moved westward before the white population, and took possession in the limestone districts. In these comparatively low tracts they found an abundance of good grass in summer, and many places over-grown with bullrushes, together with the fine buffalo-grass, supplied them with winter food; salt water is found on the confines of the limestone, and there are several well-known salt licks where the buffalo were sure to be found; at all seasons of the year they wandered constantly from place to place, either from being disturbed by hunters or in quest of food.

They were much attracted by the soft, tender grass which springs up after a fire has spread over the prairies. They were generally very shy, and took to flight instantly on scenting the hunter; they were less wary when assembled together in numbers, and would often follow their leader regardless of or trampling down the hunters posted in their way.

Herds of buffalo wandered over the middle and western counties as late as '72, usually led by one remarkable for strength and fierceness. While feeding they would scatter over a great extent of country; but when moving they formed a dense and almost impenetrable column, which once in motion could scarcely be impeded even by rivers, across which they swam, without fear or hesitation nearly in the order they traversed the plains. When fleeing before their pursuers it would be in vain for the foremost to halt or attempt to obstruct the progress of the main body. As the throng in the rear advance, destruction awaited the foremost, unless they rushed pell-mell over the prairie. The flesh of the buffalo, when in good condition, especially the calves, is very sweet, juicy, and well flavored, much resembling well-fed beef. I have eaten the flesh of the buffalo calf that was as sweet and tender as young chicken. I have seen wagon loads of the meat enroute for market, each wagon drawn by several yoke of Texas oxen; but they have been slaughtered for their meat, their hides to make robes, and for mere sport, until at the present time, their numbers are few in Kansas; if any they are in the extreme western counties.

The time the massacre took place, of which I have given a picture, and of which I write in particular, was in 1869. At that time a considerable supply of the settler's meat was obtained from that source. There being no buffalo in the northern counties, east of the Republican river, in Republic County, they must necessarily go eighty or one hundred miles to find plenty of game.

In May, 1869, a party of seven, consisting of J. L. McChesney, a Mr. Cole and son, an uncle and cousin of Mr. M's., Phillip Burk, an ex-union soldier, Ruban Winklepleck and son, also a nephew of Mr. W., started from Waterville. Buffalo were not found until they had reached the head waters of White Rock, a tributary of the Republican; there they found the untamed monsters of the prairie in abundance. In a few days they succeeded in bringing down enough to load their wagons; also caught a calf, which Mr. Cole was going to take to Michigan as a curiosity.

They commenced their homeward journey in good spirits over their excellent success in hunting, little thinking the dark savage with eyes full of vicious hate, was ploting their capture and destruction. A scouting party of Cheyennes had discovered them, and like the sly, sneaking coyotes of the prairie, they were planning their fiendish raid. The hunting party, unconscious of the impending danger, leisurely traveled down the stream, seeking a fording place.

The day previous to the massacre, a small party of Indians made their appearance on a distant bluff. They approached near enough to ascertain the exact strength of the hunting party, so they could capture them without any trouble. After seeing the Indians, the owner of one wagon threw his meat overboard, liberated the buffalo calf and made the best speed possible. The ammunition of the hunters was nearly gone, and any firing on their part would be useless. They were nearing the mouth of White Rock and must necessarily cross the Republican. Near the junction of the two streams was an old log fort, built by

the soldiers years before. Night was coming on; they did not dare to travel with their
teams after dark. A council was held, and
they resolved to reach the fort and pass the
night, thinking, perhaps, help might arrive.
There they passed the night. Some pro-
posed to abandon their teams and under
cover of darkness make their escape, if
possible, on foot; but that looked too cowardly for an old soldier like Mr. Burk, for not
more than a half a dozen Indians had been
seen.

Morning came. If attacked at the fort
they were helpless, as their ammunition was
nearly gone. The Indians were not in sight.
They resolved to harness and start for the
Republican to find a fording place. Mr. M.
traveled on foot to ascertain something def-
inite about the ford, as the stream was dangerous even at low water; that gave him one
chance out of one hundred for escape.

They reached the river at a point where
the logs for the fort had been hauled up

the bank, when with the rapidity of a meteor there sprang from the very sand, as it appeared, about one hundred Indians, all mounted and armed to the teeth, with guns, arrows and tomahawks, yelling like demons from the infernal pit. They surrounded the doomed party, shooting their bullets and arrows, which seemed to fill the very air. The party sprang from their wagons, abandoning everything, while the air fairly shrieked with the bullets and flying arrows; they plunged into the river (with the exception of Mr. M.), making a desperate effort cross the swollen stream.

The blood-thirsty savages hotly pursued; the hunters saw no chance of escape unless they could cross the river and a narrow strip of prairie on the opposite bank, and then reach the timber beyond. If they could accomplish that they had some hopes, thinking they could secrete themselves among the trees, brush, weeds and grass. They made the attempt; all crossed the river, reached the open prairie, when the Indians overtook them, killing the six. Two were residents of Michigan, visiting relatives in Kansas.

At first Mr. M. succeeded in secreting himself in the tall weeds and tangled grass in such a manner that about twenty Indians who were searching for him passed within six feet of his body. He could see their vicious, fiery eyes peering over the weeds and grass which concealed him. He could see their guns ready to riddle him with bullets, and the uplifted tomahawk ready to take his scalp; their horses almost trod upon his clothing. Mr. M. knew all that was going on upon the opposite bank of the river, when the savages were killing his comrades, by their unearthly yells; their tomahawks soon silenced all else, and he could not distinguish a familiar voice.

After they had completed their bloody deed, he heard them sing their savage song of rejoicing. Mr. M. succeeded in getting away from his concealment and was followed four miles, but the Indians would not abandon their horses and Mr. M. crept slily from place to place until they relinquished their search entirely; then he succeeded in reaching Scandia, fifteen miles distant, where he procured a posse and started for the scene of the massacre. They found them all dead—all scalped but one. Two stripped of all their clothing, their bodies filled with bullets. One arrow was taken from the body of Mr. W. and taken to Michigan, as a memento of the horrible scene.

Mr. McChesney's escape seems almost incredible, and next to a miracle; but he is an honorable man, highly respected, and has lived in Kansas almost a quarter of a century, and his veracity has never been questioned; I received this statement from him.

Kansas as I Heard it in 1867.

WIFE, I've concluded the prairies to see;
 Our children are young, and our acres
  are few,
 We'll go to the west, where cattle roam
  free,
 And I'll take a homestead, as other
  men do.

Some of our neighbors are going next fall;—
 There's Baker, and Brown and William-
  son, too;
 They've been out to Kansas,
  And looked the state through.

Scene in Northern Kansas in 1873.

Residence of Hon. Charles F. Koester, Mashall Co., Kansas.

The prairies are rolling, and covered with
    flowers.
They say it is lovely, the grass grows so
    high,—
And better than all, no doctor to pay;
    For there it's so healthy, that men never
    die.

Uncle Sam, you know, for a very small sum,
    Will give me a farm, that nature made
    clear.
I'll build me a house, and break up my land,
    And then I'll be worth more'n a dozen
    men here.

Now, wife, we'll plan, and talk of our trip,
    Of our overland journey, and camping out,
    too.
We'll build up our fire, by the road-side at
    night,
    And eat on the ground, as other folks do.

We'll sell what we can, and the rest give
    away,

For when we are there, we've nothing to
    fear,
Our potatoes and corn will grow without
    work,
And we'll feast on sweet buffalo half of
    the year.

They say those plains have the rarest of
    game,
There's the buffalo, elk and antelope, too;
While the grass is filled with chicken and
    quail,
And there is the turkey that weighs
    twenty-two.

I'll put in my crops, and go hunting, you
    know,
While you mind the children, and live at
    your ease.
No smudges to build, the mosquitoes to
    scare;
No potatoes to bury, for there they won't
    freeze.

Now, wife, we will dream of that land of
  delight,
How we'll gather the flowers that cover
  the lea;
That fertile vale, with fountains so clear,
  That cherished home this fall, we will see.

Kansas as it is.

ANSAS is a noted state,
  With many thriving towns,
But like all other states, you know,
  She has her ups and downs.

Kansas yet is young in years,
  But not ashamed of her acres tilled;
Nor of the stock she sends abroad;
  Nor of her cribs, her corn has filled.

She's rich in mines of zinc and lead;
  And coal is found of every hue,
Her gypsum mills grind up her rocks,
  That makes your old land new.

Farm Residence of Capt. Joseph Wilson and Son, in Northern Kansas, in 1883.

Her schools are good as can be found
 In any other place
Old teachers have to scratch around
 To keep themselves in pace
Our boys sixteen are bound to win—
 They'll head them in the race.

Her soil is sought, I do aver,
 By thirty states, or more,
And foreigners, from every port,
 Have landed on her shore,

Of all the states that ere have been,
 Since we from Britain's yoke was free,
The state of Kansas leads the van,
 As you will plainly see.

Sketch.

———

THE BURNING AND SACKING OF LAWRENCE BY QUANTRELL THE GUERRILLA CHIEFTAIN.

———

THE annexed view of Lawrence in 1863, during the inhuman and barbarous raid of the rebels under Quantrell, is taken from a drawing and sketch given by one who miraculously escaped the scorching flames, bloody knife, and fatal ball of the raiders. A very brief sketch was collected by historians and passed into history, but the true picture of the scene has never been depicted,—perhaps never will be.

Burning and Sacking of Lawrence, by Quantrell, in 1863.

The massacre of Lawrence appears in the
minds of the young men of to-day as an idle
tale, not as a real, cold-blooded murdering,
done by American sons—men who received
their education under the stars and stripes,
which waves one destiny. A community
would expect nothing else of the untamed,
blood-thirsty savages, only to attack defense-
less families and towns, shoot and tomahawk on the spot, or satiate their wild, un-
civilized mind by torturing with slow fire,
and aggravating their prisoners with their
wild dance and hideous yells; but it seems
almost incredible that American sons, nurtured under this government, schooled in its
free institutions of learning, should do such
diabolical deeds! But, nevertheless, it is
true, as all of the ablest generals who raised
their fratricidal hands, and uttered the vilest
threats against our country, were West
Point graduates! It nurtured the vipers that
were to open their mouths and hiss out the
envenomed poison that was to fill the dense

woods, hills, ravines and trenches with the noble, loved and patriotic sons of American mothers!

If the heart sickening sight of the Lawrence massacre, together with the cells in Libby, Castle Thunder, Salisbury and other pens could be hung up in one bold panorama, so the young men of to-day could gaze upon it, they would cry out in horror, "is it possible that American sons endured such imprisonment, such vile torture, such detestable hardships?"

When the arch-angel shall sound his trumpet, legions will be the number that will come forth, that were made way with in the dark days of rebellion, that are to history, and our country at large, as though they had never been. For instance: while traveling through this state, several years ago I was pointed out a place in Lima county (by an ex-union soldier), where nine men were shot in cold blood; their only crime being they chose to have the free soil of Kansas untrampled by oppressors. Scores of such black deeds are not recorded which ought to be, so the young men could read and take warning of the past, and choose that which will attain to true greatness, having respect for their fellow mortals, whether of high or low degree; and by knowing the worst prevent, if possible, future rebellions.

The history they read is considered the depository of events, the faithful evidence of truth, the source of prudence and good counsel. As it is history that sets all the actions, achievements, virtues and faults of men in high standing before their eyes, and sets a mark of infamy on vices which no after age can obliterate, it tends to strengthen our abhorence of vice, and creates an honorable ambition for the attainments of true greatness, and solid glory; therefore, it ought to throw off the mask altogether, and bring to light the unjust, unlawful, abuse of those in the past holding or usurping power over their fellow mortals.

There had been repeated alarms that the
rebels were coming, which proved false, con-
sequently they were thrown off their guard
and entirely unprepared to defend themselves
against a body of savage guerrillas, conseq-
uently the citizens of the doomed city were
surprised at dawn of day on the 21st of
August, 1863, the enemy, rushing into the
city, instantly setting fire to the buildings,
shooting those they met first and leaving
them weltering in their blood, while they
rushed savagely on to their work of destruction and death. Women and children were
terrified; men were helpless because they
were surprised and overpowered by a band
whose only terms was cold lead and the
glittering knife. The roar of the flames, as
they leaped from the once peaceful dwell-
ings, the crashing of falling timber; the yelling and unceasing oaths of the raiders; the
crack of revolvers, as they laid loved ones
low in death; the clatter of hoofs, as the
raiders rode hither and thither on their

fiendish work of death and despoilation; the awful appearance of destruction and woe, mingled with the dreadful shrieks of women and children; the groans of the dying and wounded; exhibited a most horrid and affecting scene, a scene too great for men to behold who were bred in the quiet retirements of domestic life. The scene presented after the raiders left was enough to appal the stoutest heart. Buildings burned to the ground, the street strewn with wounded and dead, scores of children who had been made orphans, crying for those whose spirits had flown to that undiscovered country, from whose bourn no traveler returns, those that had escaped, left destitute of food and clothing, all combined presented a spectcle which no tongue can describe, nor pen portray.

Burning and Sacking of Lawrence.

———•——•◦○%○◦•——•———

CALM and peaceful was the morning,
   When that rebel chieftain wild,
Said, "I'll burn the town of Lawrence—
   Murder man, woman and child!

" 'Tis the twenty-first of August;—
   History soon will note the day,
When the rebels, under Quantrell,
   Captured Lawrence for their prey.

"My men are thirsting for the blood
   Of loyal sons on Kansas soil!
Such deeds are cowardly, I know;—
   They make the devil shrink and coil.

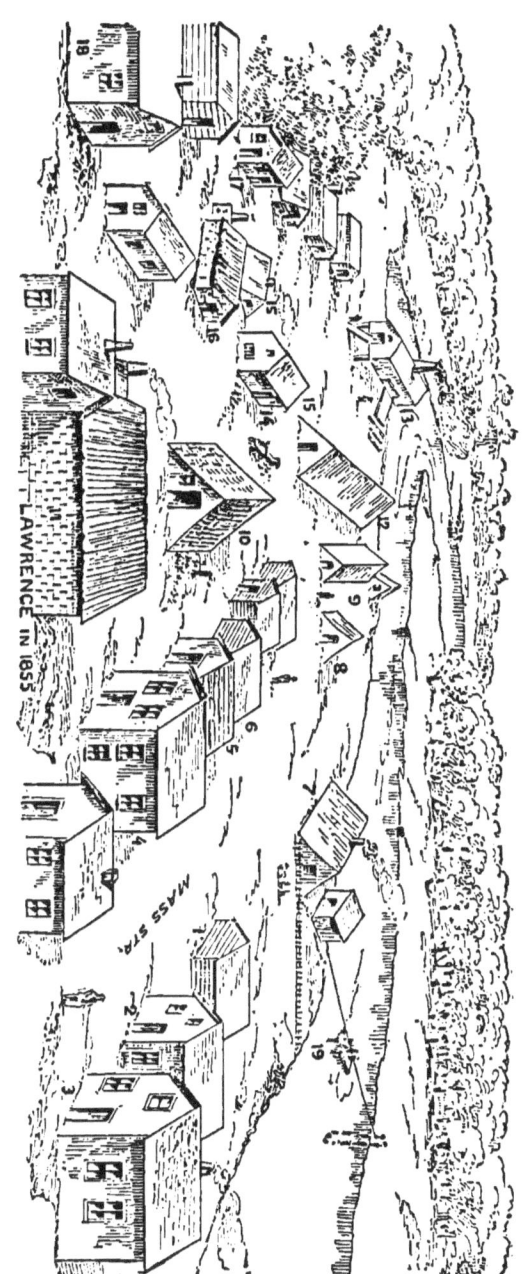

LAWRENCE IN 1855

MASS STR.

1 First House in Lawrence.
2 Kansas "Free State" Office.
3 "Herald of Freedom" Office.
4 Emigrant Aid Office.
5 The 1st Post Office   E. W. Babcock, P.M.
6 S. N. Simpson's Land Office and 1st Sabbath Scho ll.
7 Hoyt's Residence.
8 Ex-Gov. C. Robinson's Office.
9 Pioneer Hotel, Litchfield & Burson, Propr's.
10 Sands' Harness Shop.
11 Chas. Stearns' Eating House.

12 First Church.
13 Emigrant Aid Mill.
14 T. Simpson's Meat Market.
15 S. N. Simpson's Residence.
16 St. Nicholas Hotel, S. Fry, Prop.
17 Miller & Elliott's Printing Office.
18 S. & F. Kimball's Residence.
19 Ferry on Kansas River.
20 John Speer's Residence.
21 Kansas Tribune.

"But blood's our prey, and blood we'll have;
  Our horses' hoofs be red with gore!
We've murdered for opinion's sake,
  And now we'll murder as before.

"We'll plan our raid before we start;
  We'll divide our force in numbers three—
So we can capture every man;—
  But Quantrell will your leader be.

"We will not spare; we'll burn the town!
  Grim monster death mark out our track.
We'll show them that no northern sons
  Must tamper with our stock in black.

"We'll subdue those loyal sons,
  From Kansas unto Maine;
For, Cole, you heard our leaders say,
  They're bound to have the reign.

"Make ready now and we will go;
  We're bound to rule with knife and lead;
We were not born to till the soil—
  Our aim is to sup at the fountain head."

Away they start from their lurking place;
  They reached the town ere it it was light.
They did not meet a well-drilled force,
  Nor troops prepared to give them fight.

But helpless ones, whose eyes were closed
  In peaceful slumbers of the night,
Who did not think, ere all arose,
  Their town would be one ghastly sight.

The word was caught, 'twas, "there they
      come!"
The bengal beast leaped from his lair.
Oh! will he kill without remorse
  The infant on its mother's breast,
The aged one with silvered hair?

They touched the match to buildings all,
  The flames went bursting here and there;
And then the shrieks of wounded men
  Pierced wildly through the morning air.

They with stoutest hearts, shrank to see
  The intense suffering and the woe

Blue Rapids Falls, Blue Rapids, Kansas.

That was inflicted on that town
  By Quantrell's band the—rebel foe!

Men, women, children, all alike,
  Sought refuge from that rebel band,
Who, with the power of Bonaparte,
  Would lay in ashes all our land.

The frightful flames were bursting loud,
  And leaping wildly through the air,
As if to add to the piteous shrieks
  That rose and fell in sore despair.

The father, with his darling sons,
  The mother, with her child,
Cried, "burn my house, but spare my life!'
  Those shrieks were loud and wild!

And helpless children did behold
  Those fiends in human form
Shoot down their fathers in the street,
  With unrelenting scorn'

The butchering done by Quantrell's band,
  Upon that Autumn day,

Will, like a dagger, pierce my heart—
So they who saw it say.

Killing men had made him brave;—
    Bnt there his ire grew wild
When Younger said, "you made a vow;—
    You've missed part of your game!"
And then he gnashed his teeth in rage,
    And said, "I'll shoot Jim Lane!"

Ah! sad was the fate of Lawrence that day,.
    As the panting steed bore his rider in gray,
As their curses, shrieks and deafening cries
    Were wafted upward to the skies.

When that awful day had past,
    Smoldering ruins marked the spot
Where love and friendship reigned supreme,
    Ere Quantrell planned his bloody plot.

But a mark of infamy is set
    On the men who plotted treason;
Who thought to rend our land in twain,
    Without just cause or reason.

And now o'er the graves of New England's
    sons,
O'er the martyrs who fell that day,
Year following year, the tear-drops will fall
    On the ground that has mixed with their
    clay.

To the
Memory of the Hon. D. G. Haskell.

———————<><>%<><>———————

TO-DAY the nation mourns a son,
    In early life he was cut down.
    Our friend, our guide, when noon had
        past:—
    No words can speak a woe so vast!

His years were few, but well-improved;—
    He gained a coveted renown,
And stamped upon the nation's mind
    That he has gained a heavenly crown.

Long had sickness on him preyed;
    Anxious friends had watched each mail,

While round his bead a loving wife
In sorrow heard each changing tale.

His voice—that was true to his country—
No more will be heard through the halls
When congress assembles for duty,—
Where justice should ring o'er its walls.

This is a privilege all may speak—
A sacred grief where all had part;—
Where sorrow saddened every brow,
And flowed through every aching heart.

Kansas wept; her grief was great.
She mourned a son, noble, kind, true and
serene.
He stayed!—we watched the uncertain
doom.
He fell!—what mourning clothed the
scene!

Pale on his couch the sufferer lay;
'Twas a weary battle-ground of pain.

Love watched his pillow: science tried
    Her every art—but all, alas! in vain!

Ah! could the grief of all that mourned
    Blend in one voice its solemn cry,
The wail would reach from shore to shore;
    The echo sound from sky to sky.

'Twas not our nation to decide
    Whom death shall claim, or skill shall
        save.
Though Haskell's life by God denied,
    It gave our state a noble grave.

Farewell! farewell to that noble son!
    We wonder why he was cut down;—
But Enoch walked with God, we're told,
    And at noon was borne into the fold.

PART II.

PATRIOTIC.

Sketch.

THE scene presented on the following page took place during the war. It was during Gen. Thomas' exciting and momentous campaign in the mountains of Tennessee.

There were many times when it was feared their hour had come; their communications were frequently cut off and the whole command was in danger of certain destruction.

They were intrenched upon a spur of the hills around Chatanooga, where they had been driven by the desperate courage of the Confederates. Their store of provisions had run low, and but one line of communication was left open to them—that of the railroad in the eastern part of the state. By a flank movement the Confederates succeeded in putting a line across the last highway; thus they were hemmed in; starvation or surrender stared them in the face; one alternative or the other must be accepted in a few days, unless some unexpected change took place.

Gen. Thomas grew hourly pale and despairing; he thought the fate perhaps of a nation was depending upon his action; but he was not the man to yield until every resource had been sounded to the bottom, and there was one resource left, and that was desperate and almost hopeless.

Forty miles to the eastward of them lay Stockton's command of nearly 30,000 men, unconscious of the terrible danger awaiting both commands. Stockton's command had been directed to occupy a pass in the mountains on the left, and to hold it until further orders. Of course, unaware of the terrible condition of the main army, he would make no movement for their relief.

Communications were now entirely cut off, and it seemed an utter impossibility to re-open them through the heavy line of Confederates which lay across the railroad. Thomas, however, determined to try it, and selected three resolute and tried men from that noble army for the dangerous, but honorable, duty.

They had reason to believe that the enemy had not destroyed the railroad, and if not captured at the outset they might succeed in taking an engine through to Kanakia Station, where Stockton, with his command, lay.

All things ready and orders given at 10:30 they mounted the engine that was to carry them to death, or save an army. Before starting, the engineer ordered two tallow cans to be put on board as he was going to make time and expected the machine would heat up finely; the cans were stowed away in the caboose, the engineer opened the throttle-valve; amidst an impressive silence of the soldiers surrounding the starting point they slowly moved away. They passed the first battery and were under the guns of two more. The works at that point had been constructed to command the junction of a union line with another running south. There was also a station at that point, and as they whirled passed they saw an engine standing on a side-track with steam up; they also caught sight of a number of men running toward it and others busy with the car, but going as they were at break-neck speed it was impossible for them to ascertain the cause of the bustle, but they found out too soon. They were preparing to give them a chase, and capture them if possible !

"Now They Were Chasing Them Almost in Sight"   p. 54.

Taking a Message Through.

———◦◦◇◈◇◦◦———

A N army waiting anxiously,
    With alternate hopes and fears,
  To see what they can do;—
    With communication all cut off,
  Who'll take a message through?

Three men with nerve and stalwart frames,
    Who were loyal, brave and true,
  Were chosen from that motley crowd,
    To take a message through.

The road was guarded, here and there,
    With pickets, scouts, and batteries, too;

So they must expect naught else but death
    If they try to take a message through!

The engine was cleaned and prepared for the
        trip,
    Till her sound little works looked bright
        and new;
And now for the cause she would do her
        best,
    And that was all that an engine could do.

They bid farewell, then mounted the cab;—
    No one would choose their work to do,
But the life of an army was at stake—
    They'll die, or take a message through!

And then from the midst of that silent crowd
    They slowly moved away,
And soon they came to a well-known spot
    Where a rebel battery lay.

Then missiles of death were hurled at them;
    'Twas a storm of shot and shell and grape;

They cared not how or where they fell,
 So they hit in any shape.

"More fire!" was the word from the engineer,
 "We must try those irons to miss;—
For if the rebs should hit their mark,
 We'll fire no more in this!"

They passed by battery number one;
 Their loss was small, as they could tell:
To them it was a useless piece of brass,
 And left by the wayside where it fell.

One battery was passed but there were two
 more.
 The shrieking iron then filled the air!
"Fill up the furnace, or we are done—
 There's no hope but in despair!"

Just then a shell—a monster—struck them,
 Crushed through the cab, broke the fire-
 man's arm;
He groaned "who'll fire the rest of the trip?"

Your comrade, for that shell has done him
    no harm.

"They're safe!" they said, with a sigh of re-
    lief;
    They'd passed their last works, their road
        now was clear,
But the fireman groaned "we ain't through
    with it yet;
    The worst is to come—they are following,
        I fear!"

They looked at the man, and thought he was
    crazed;
    But listning intently found out he was
        right.
They had pulled out the engine they passed
    on the track;
    Now they were chasing them—almost in
        sight!

The furnace was kept to its highest heat,
    Till the boiler wheazed and groaned for
        breath;

The wheels spun around upon the track—
It seemed like sure and certain death!

"More fire, more fire!" said the engineer.
"They're gaining on us fast!" he cried.
And then he opened the furnace door,
    And cramed it full from side to side.

"Is there naught else that we can do?
    Try something quick to stop their speed!
Let's throw a bar across the track!"
    To which they quickly all agreed.

Again they came with redoubled speed!
    "Here, throw a coat across the track!"
The coat was caught—but I shrink to tell,
    'Twas only a moment it kept them back.

Again they come, fierce and faster than
        before,
    The engine emitting great clouds of smoke.
Just then they knew not what to do,
    When thus the thoughtful fireman spoke:

"Where are those cans we put aboard?
　Brave John, that's just the thing; no one
　　　but you
Would thought of the like to grease the
　　　track,
　That we might take a message through!"

The cans were brought and the rails were
　　　oiled;
　Their pursuers rushed onto the glistning
　　　track,
But instead of the prize they expected to get
　The wheels rolled round and the car went
　　　back.

Their car rolled on till a shot was fired,
　And then they saw our boys in blue,
They're safe beneath the stars and stripes,
　They'd lived to take the message through!

Lincoln's Call for Troops.

HERE are the thousands—seventy-five—
 Whom Abram loudly first did call?
 Say, were they mustered out with you,
 Or were they covered with a pall?
 Oh! where are they?

Again he said in sixty-one,
 "Our blood bought land our fathers' won
As sons we must defend;—
 Some forty thousand stalwart ones
Must lend a helping hand."
 Oh! where are they?

Again he said, with a troubled mind,
 "The foe is on our track!

Three hundred thousand more I'll call,
    To beat the oppressors back."
        Oh! where are they?

Again he said, in sixty-two,
    "Our country must not fall!
It grieves me sore to think I must
    Three hundred thousand call."
        Oh! where are they?

And yet he saw 'twas their intent
    Our nation to destroy; and as he took his
        pen
Three hundred thousand more to call
    He said, "my country, can it be
That these brave boys must fall?"
        Oh! where are they?

In four months more, with a weary frame,
    And a heart that felt for all,
He said, "five hundred thousand more must
        come;
    Will they answer to my call?"
        Oh! where are they?

Again he said, "we will be crushed
  Without two hundred thousand more!"
And then they rallied from the hills of Maine,
  And from the bleeding Kansas shore.
      Oh! where are they?

Stout hearts recoiled from the bloody strife,
  That traitorous sons brought on;
Five hundred thousand more must come
  Before the victory's won.
      Oh! where are they?

With throbbing heart and anxious brow,
  Again our leader said:
"The foe that's drenched our land with blood,
  They cannot hold out long;—
So come and help the weary ones—
  Three hundred thousand strong!"
      Oh! where are they?

And so they went—two million men—
  And many thousand more,

To show to all the world around
   That poisonous tree with deadly fruit,
Was uprooted on our shore.
            Oh! where are they?

Died at Stone River.

When traitors struck this mighty nation
　　Such a blow her temple trembled,
　Abram called her loyal sons;—
　　From the north they soon assembled
　To meet her bold, rebellious ones.

Among the troops that volunteered
　Was a fair and lovely one,
A treasure of a northern household—
　A boy sixteen, an only son.

The word to come was quickly given
　That tore the household wreaths apart;
Mothers tried to bear the anguish,
　Strove to shield a noble heart.

In that sad and lonely dwelling,
A mother pressed her darling boy,
Upon his cheek she placed a kiss
In his hand she placed a token:
"Where ere you go you'll think of this;

"Go my son, your country calls.
'Tis not for fame nor shining gold,
But to shield our blood-bought liberty
Our fathers won in days of old!"

The sad good bys were quickly given,
The train went speeding through the air,
Some it bore from home forever,
Some a prison pen to share.

Loyal hearts will all remember,
When they nobly took the field,
'Twas that beautiful September,
And the war trump's loudly pealed!

Oh! how grand they seemed while passing
To the front, where troops were massing;

Loyal from disloyal classing.
　Brothers of one mighty nation,
Accursed slavery rent assunder;—
　For it the innocent did suffer.
Where shells did burst and cannons thunder.

They were passing scenes, enchanting
　Scenes, which some would see no more.
Then they joined the third division,
　Third brigade and fourteenth corps;—

And they won some gems worth naming,
　Honors true and nobly gaining
For themselves, reward maintaining,
　And their nation's flag sustaining.

Through Kentucky and the wilds of Tenn-
　essee,
　Where with Buell as commander,
They assumed supremacy.
　At Mill Spring, and Pittsburg Landing,
And other points they won renown,

Till Stanton said "you're superceeded,
  You must lay your saber down.!"

Then with Rosy as commander,
  They, the patriotic host,
Prepared to meet that rebel leader,
  That was known from coast to coast.

In the fight, when stout hearts faltered,
  Shrank from the outnumbering host,
Among the sons that bled for freedom,
  Died ere they would leave their post,
Was that true and noble one.

At the first he missed the bullets,
  While at his side his comrades fell;
But ere the sound of victory echoed
  Through the woods and down the dell,
A ball had struck him, and he faltered—
  Called a comrade ere he fell:—

"Bear a message to my mother—
  Lo! she waits to hear from me—

That I filled the post of duty,
  From the foe did never flee!

"Tell her I was in the battle,
  In the thickest of the fight;
The foe was fighting for secession,—
  We were battling for the right.

"I am wounded, deeply wounded,
  For my country's sake I've fell;
This will bring you years of sorrow,
  For it is my last farewell!

"I will bear the last great struggle,
  That which mortals fear and dread,
If you'll always say of treason,
  Crush that fiery serpent's head!

"Do not break your heart with weeping;
  I will trust the gracious giver.
The hand of death is o'er me creeping,—
  I am dying on Stone River!"

Battle of Wilson Creek and Death of Gen. Lyon.

———◦◦◦◦❦◦●●———

'TWAS on the first of August,
  That well-remembered day,
When Lyon, with his little band,
  From Springfield marched away.

The ditches were all filled
  With our country's bitter foes,
On the Banks of Wilson Creek,
  Where McCulloch did repose.

He'd scoured the country far and wide,
  Over prairie, grove and glen;
He'd robbed alike both friend and foe,
  For twenty thousand men.

Gen. Lyon's Monument, Springfield, Mo.

On the morning of the ninth
  Lyon's mind with care was pressed;
He thought to slay secession
  Before it left the nest.

He studied well his chances,
  Ere the rising of the sun,
For the rebs did him outnumber
  Full three to every one.

With the stars and stripes afloating
  Beneath the azure blue,
They marched in silence to the field,
  The loyal, brave and true.

No muffled drum was beating,
  The faintest heart to cheer,
But 'twas their country loudly called them
  To protect the west frontier.

Lyon took the front,
  While Sigel took the rear;
The time had come to try the brave,
  The loyal volunteer.

To fight for liberty,
  Our country and its laws,
Or drink the dregs of treason,
  Regardless of the flaws.

War's fearful blast they soon must share;
  The line was formed, the word was given,
The deadly bullets filled the air,
  From Totten's Battery driven.

Charge after charge that heroic band
  Drove back the rebel host,
Like waves from off the solid strand,
  On a stearn and rock-bound coast.

Where the battle raged the fiercest,
  And the bullets flew like hail,
Lyon's form was in the thickest,—
  At sight of him they would not fail.

"His horse is shot!" cried out the aid;—
  The panting steed lay dying there,
While groans and shrieks from wounded men
  In wild confusion filled the air.

"Here's another—take this charger.
He is proud of the battle's fray;
He will bear his gallant rider
Through the perils of the day!"

He grasped the rein nor lost a moment,
While smoke and bullets filled the air—
'Twas a time when General Lyon
Saw no hope, but in despair.

Then they saw a cruel bullet,
Coursing through that human tide,
Till it reached its destination,
In that gallant leader's side.

Then another, still more deadly,
Went to take an active part·—
Went to ring another life-drop
From that true and noble heart.

Then they saw the fruit of treason,—
The rebel horde had picked their game,
Then they sent another bullet,
Tearing through that mortal frame.

Then cried his men—but all in vain!—
  "Oh leave the field, you're racked with
      pain!
Go to the rear, your wounds have dressed,
  You're weak and faint, and must have
      rest."

They saw the blood drip from his brow,
  They wondered why this war must be;
When some one said Columbia's sons
  Have tried to crush our liberty.

Again they cried, "Oh! leave the field!"
  But Lyon thought he could not yield;
He saw that he was needed there
  To keep his men from deep despair.

The rebels formed in a solid mass,
  Resolved to die or win that time.
It seemed as though one puff of war
  Would sweep away the loyal line.

Lyon saw the fearful moment,
  Called unto the brave and just:—

"We must now protect that banner,
Or they'll trail it in the dust.

"They will take that noble ensign,
That for which our fathers bled;
They will rend its stripes assunder,
O'er its stars they all will tread.

"That glorious flag they trailed at Sumpter,
To plant it here our fathers died,
Now, as sons, we'll shield that banner
On the old Missouri side!"

Another charge, and who will lead,
Lyon's form is red with gore.
"Come on brave men!" he calmly said,
"My God and country I adore!"

Through the smoke they saw brave Lyon,
At the front he lead the van;
Hoping by unflinching courage,
To sweep secession from our land.

They made the charge—fought hand to hand,
   They strewed the field with rebels slain;
They won the day, but Lyon fell,
   Bleeding at every vein.

Again they heard their fiendish yell,—
   Five times they'd shot that loyal son;
Their long and vicious deadly hate
   Had stilled the heart of that noble one.

His blood poured out on southern soil,
   Where traitors cried, "Ah! give us more,
We want more room for slaves to toil,
   And bind our fetters at every door!"

They saw that crimson current flowing,
   From that true and noble one,
Where the hateful form of slavery,
   Cried, "Ah! give, Ah! give me room.

"Room to smite this land with cursing,
   Room to fetter, chain and slay,
From the trembling mother's bosom,
   Room to tear her child away.

Room to trample on the manhood
  Of this nation far and wide;
Room to spread o'er every portion
  Slavery's low, debasing tide.

When that blow it struck the nation,
  Lips compressed that scarce could tell
Of their dear and brave defender,
  How he fought and how he fell.

Loved ones heard that solemn message,
  Lo, it struck the vital part;
'Twas "Lyon is dead, our dear commander,
  A rebel bullet pierced his heart!"

Then they bore that form away,
  To that sacred hearth-stone, where
Ere that cruel war was raging,
  There arose a fervent prayer.

Loved ones will weep above that grave,
  Weep as though the heart would break,
When they know his life was taken,—
  Taken for opinion sake.

The Dying Soldier.

MARCHING for Atlanta,
 Sweeping scouts and pickets
Driving in the foe,
 With the peals of martial music,
 Did Sherman's army go.

Through forests deep and rough ravines,
 'Twas skirmish day by day,
To feel the foe and and know the point
 Where the rebel Hood did lay.

It was a grand and gorgeous sight;—
 They bore our flag on high,
As o'er the hills and through the vales
 Our boys went sweeping by.

They tried to flank them on their march,
  With solid shot and shell,
When a thousand muskets said "retreat,
  For I do my mission well."

The deep voiced thunder pealed afar,
  And strewed the ground with dead,
Till it was covered with their blood,
  And solid balls of lead.

The rebels charged again and again,
  The lines swayed to and fro,
Till flesh and blood could bear no more,
  Nor the sullen craven foe.

Then on that field of dead and dying,
  Was one so true and young in years;
His ghastly wound was plainly telling
  'Twould bring a mother's burning tears.

They saw the golden cord was loosened,
  They knew that he must die;
They could read that mournful message,
  In that calm and blood-shot eye.

They read it in the purple flow,
    That roamed from cheek to cheek,
And the quivering of his pallid lips,
    Though faint he thus did speak:

Glancing at his mangled limb,
    With a calm and tearful eye
He said, "we've gained the victory, boys!
    But comrades, I must die!"

He drew a picture from his breast,
    Then called a friend beside:—
"This is my mother; tell her all—
    'Twas for the flag I died!"

And then he pressed it to his lips,
    And said, "before I go,
We'll give three cheers for the dear old flag
    That flag will win, I know!"

Then with a gentle smile,
    His spirit winged its flight;
No more to hear the bugles call,
    Or share the bloody fight.

Decoration Day.

———◦◦◦✸◦◦◦———

'TIS mete that we should meet this day,
    And bring the rarest flowers,
And strew them on our comrades'
    graves,
    In memory of the hours
When we were called to cut the sod
    And place our comrades under:—
They who the hand of treason had
    From this world snatched assunder.

'Tis mete that we should meet this day,
    To join in songs and homage pay
To those who then with fear and wonder,
    Lest our nation be rent assunder,

Gave up their homes and loved ones dear,
  And suffering bore from year to year,
Then yielded up their lives.

'Tis mete that we should set apart
  A day of adoration,
In honor of our sons that fought
  And fell to save this nation;
And while our days are lengthened out,
  We will each year spread flowers about
Our comrade's graves.

'Tis mete that we should weld anew
  Our sacred honor and our love,
For they whose voice is hushed in death,
  Whose spirits are in heaven above;
For the boys who quietly slumber,
  In the ground so cold and damp,
The boys of our martyred army,
  The boys in the silent camp.

'Tis mete that we should teach our sons,
  All treason to abhor,

By pointing out to them each year
The misery of that war,
  That calls us here to-day, `
Our rarest flowers to display
  And strew upon their graves,

'Tis mete that we should teach our sons,
  To choose the right and shun the wrong,
And honor those who fell;
  Who bore their grief and suffering well
Our nation to sustain,
  And all its laws maintain,
And from oppression to refrain
  And live in peace with all.

And when our race on earth is done,
  And here we meet no more,
Our children will observe a day,
  Their love and flowers to display,
And strew them o'er our crumbling clay,
  As we have done.

Battle of North Point and Bombardment of Fort McHenry.

———◦◦◦◦◦———

THE author noticed an inquiry quite recently, in newspaper columns, asking who is the author of the the Star Spangled Banner, and for the benefit of those (if this book happens to fall into the hands of that class), I will insert the following account of the Battle of North Point and the Bombardment of Fort McHenry, in September 1814, which is from M'Sherry's History of Maryland:

Having triumphantly despoiled the capitol of the Union, Gen. Ross turned his eyes upon the flourshing and wealthy city of Baltimore. Anticipating his design, the

governor had ordered the militia of the
state to hold themselves in readiness, and
large bodies were marched to the city for its
defense, about seven hundred regulars, several volunteer and militia companies from
Pennsylvania and Virginia, increased their
strength to about fifteen thousand men.
They were commanded by Gen. Samuel
Smith, who had distinguished himself in the
Revolution by his gallant defense of Fort
Mifflin. One division of the army was con-
fided to Gen. Winder, the other to Gen.
Stricker. As soon as it was announced that
the British were approaching the city, the
militia irritated by the the disaster of Bald-
ensburg, and the sacking of Washington,
flocked in from all quarters in such numbers
that neither arms, ammunition nor provisions could be supplied them, and the services of many were necessarily declined.

As it was expected that the enemy would
land and attack the town from the east,
heavy batteries were erected on the high

grounds in that direction, and an entrench-
ment thrown up, in which the main body of
the militia were posted.   On the water-side
the city was defended by Fort McHenry,
garrisoned by a thousand men, under Maj.
Armistead.   Two   small   batteries   were
erected on the south side, while the chan-
nel was obstructed by a number of sunken
vessels.

On the 11th of September, 1814, the
British fleet, numbering fifty sail, entered
the mouth of the Patapsco, and on the
twelfth a force of five thousand men was
landed at North Point, fourteen miles from
Baltimore.   Gen. Stricker was ordered forward with three thousand two hundred men
to oppose their progress.   His force was
composed of the fifth regiment, under Col.
Sterrit;   the   sixth,   Col.   McDonald;   the
twenty-seventh, Lieut.-Col. Long; the thirty-
ninth, Col. Fowler; the fifty-first, Col. Amey;
one hundred and fifty riflemen, under Capt.
Dyer; one hundred and forty cavalry, under

Liet.-Col. Biays; and the union artillery
with six field pieces. In the regiments of
this brigade were incorporated Spangler's
York, Metzgar's Hanover, Dixon's Marietta
and Quantril's Hagerstown, uniformed vol-
unteers. He took a position about eight
miles from the city, his right resting on Bear
Creek and his left covered by a marsh; the
fifth and twenty-seventh regiments formed
the first line; the fifty-first was posted three
hundred yards in the rear of the fifth, and
the thirty-ninth in the rear of the twenty-
seventh; the sixth was held in reserve. The
artillery, six four-pounders, was planted in
the center on the main road, and a corps of
riflemen pushed in advance as skirmishers.
The rifles soon fell in with the van of the
enemy, and a sharp skirmish ensued, in
which the British Commander-in-chief, Gen.
Ross, was killed. Col. Brook, the second
in command, still continued to advance, and
at half-past three, the action commenced
with the main body by a heavy cannonade.

Gen. Stricker ordered his artillery to cease, until the enemy should get within close can-nister range, and brought up the thirty-ninth on the left of the twenty-seventh, while the first was ordered to form at right-angles with the line, resting its right near the left of the thirty-ninth. The fifty-first in attempting to execute this order, fell into confusion, which, however, was soon rem-edied. The enemy now advanced upon the twenty-seventh and thirty-ninth and the action became general. The fifty-first hav-ing imperfectly recovered from its confusion, failed to keep its ground, and having de-livered a scattering fire, broke in disorder. Its retreat threw the second battalion of the thirty-ninth into some confusion; but the whole line, undismayed by the desertion of the fifty-first, maintained its ground with the greatest firmness, pouring in a destructive fire upon the advancing columns of the enemy. The artillery opened with terrible effect upon their left, which was opposed to

the fifth, while that gallant regiment proudly
sustained the laurels it had won at Baldens-
burg.   This close and hot fire was kept up
without intermission for nearly an hour, in
the face of a foe more than treble their numbers; for the American line reduced by the
desertion of the fifty-first, and unaided by
the sixth in reserve, numbered only fourteen
hundred men.   Their volleys were deadly,
for they fired not only by order, but each
man at his mark, and the front ranks of the
enemy were frequently observed throwing
themselves upon the ground to avoid its un-
erring destruction.   Finding that his force un-
covered on its left flank, was no longer able
to make head against the superior strength
of the enemy, and having accomplished the
main object of his detachment, by the severe check he had given them, Gen. Stricker
ordered his line to retire to the position of the
sixth, his reserve regiment; this was accomplished in good order, but the fatigued condition of the troops who had been in action,

and the exposed position which he occupied, determined the General to fall back still nearer the city; the enemy, crippled by the severe contest, did not attempt pursuit; and the brigade, feeling that it had gathered the benefits of a victory, assumed a position near the lines, panting for another struggle with the invaders.

Although the American loss was heavy, it bore no comparison to that of the enemy. Adjutant James Lowry Donaldson, a member of the legislature, fell in the hottest of the conflict.   Lieut. Andre was killed; Capt. Quantril of Hagerstown, Capt. Stewart, Maj. Moore, Lieut. Reese, Joseph R. Brooks and Ensign Kirby were wounded.   Maj. Heath was wounded, and had two horses killed under him.   The American loss was twenty-four killed, one hundred and thirty nine wounded, and fifty prisoners, a total of two hundred and thirteen.

The loss of the enemy was nearly twice as great; and among their killed was their leader, Gen. Ross, who in conjunction with the notorious Cockburn, was the destroyer of the Capitol, and who had boasted that he would take up his winter quarters in Baltimore.

On the morning of the 13th of September, the British made their appearance within two miles of the intrenchments on the Philadelphia road, as if endeavoring to gain the flank of the American position; but baffled by the skillful maneuvers of Gen. Smith, after throwing forward a reconnoisance and threatening the lines in front, they retired toward their former position, deterred from the attempt by the strength of the works. Having thus failed to take the city by land, the enemy hoped that an attack by water would be more successful, and on the evening of the 13th, the fleet began to bombard the fort, its main defense, the garrison was composed of three companies of United States' artillery, and three volunteer city companies, under Capt. Berry, Lieut. Pennington and Capt. Nicholson, besides six hundred infantry, in all about one thousand men, under Col. Armistead. For a time the brave garrison were compelled to receive the fire of the fleet in silence, anchored as it was, two miles from the fort, and beyond the reach of its guns. At length, however, some confusion being created in the south-west bastion by the bursting of a bomb, several vessels were brought within range to follow up the supposed advantage; but the batteries immediately opened upon them with such effect that they were driven back to their former position. At this safe distance they poured a continuous storm of shells upon the gallant defenders of the fort, who held their posts in stern silence, ready to repulse any nearer approach.

During the night, several rocket vessels and barges, with fourteen hundred men, supplied with scaling ladders, passed silently by the fort and entered the Patapsco, little dreaming of the resistance of the six and ten-gun batteries. The foe already reveled in anticipation in the plunder of the captured city, when suddenly, as they drew opposite the six-gun battery, Lieut. Webster, its commander, opened upon them with terrible effect; the fort and the ten-gun battery also poured in their fire, and for two hours a furious cannonade was kept up, while the heavens were lighted up with the fiery courses of the bombs from the fleet and barges. The havoc was dreadful, one of the barges was sunk, and the cries of the wounded and dying could be plainly heard upon the shore. The rest, in utmost confusion, and having suffered a heavy loss, retreated precipitately to the fleet, thus baffled by land and water.

Admiral Cockburn and Col. Brooke determined to abandon the expedition; the troops were embarked on the 15th, and on the 16th, the hostile fleet dropped down the Chesapeake, leaving the liberated city filled with joy at her triumphant preservation, mingled with sorrow for the gallant sons who had died to defend her. The gallant defense of Baltimore saved the other Atlantic cities from attack, and proved to them that when led by brave and skillful officers, they need not dread to encounter any equal force of their vetran enemy.

The celebrated poem, "The Star Spangled Banner," was written by Francis S. Key, a lawyer of Baltimore. At the time of the bombardment of Fort McHenry, he had been sent with a flag of truce to Admiral Cockburn, to effect the release of some captive friends, and was himself detained on board of a cartel until after the attack. The boat was anchored in a position which enabled him and his companions to see distinctly the flag of Fort McHenry on the deck of the vessel, he remained on deck during the night, watching every shell from the moment it was fired until it fell, listening with breathless interest to hear if any explosion followed. While the bombardment continued, it was

sufficient proof that the fort had not surrendered, but it suddenly ceased, sometime
before day, and as they had no communication with any of the enemy's ships, they did
not know whether the fort had surrendered,
or the attack had been abandoned; they
paced the deck for the remainder of the
night in painful suspense. As soon as it was
light enough to discern objects at a distance,
their glasses were turned to the fort, uncertain whether they should see there the
stars and stripes or the flag of the enemy.
At length the light came and they saw that
our flag was still there.

The "Star Spangled Banner" was commenced on the deck of the vessel in the
fervor of the moment when the enemy were
seen retreating to their ships. Some brief
notes were written on the back of a letter;
for some lines he was obliged to rely on his
memory, and the whole was finished in the
boat on the way to the shore, and written
out as it now stands, at the hotel, on the

night he reached Baltimore, and immediately
after he arrived, this outburst of the patriot
and poet's heart thrilled through the souls of
great men, they took it up; it swelled from
millions of voices, and the Star Spangled
Banner became the proud national anthem
of the whole union.

The Star-Spangled Banner.

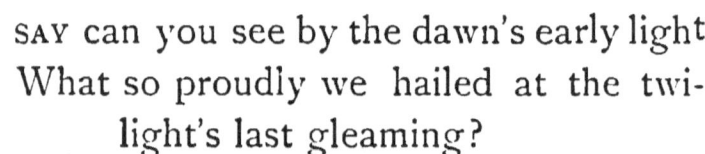

SAY can you see by the dawn's early light
What so proudly we hailed at the twilight's last gleaming?
Whose broad stripes and bright stars through
the perilous fight,
O'er the ramparts we watched were so gal-
lantly streaming!
And the rocket's red glare, the bombs bursting in air,

Gave proof through the night that our flag
was still there;
O, say, does that star-spangled banner yet
wave
O'er the land of the free and the home of
the brave?

On that shore, dimly seen through the mists
of the deep,
Where the foe's haughty host in dread silence reposes,
What is that which the breeze, o'er the towering steep,
As it fitfully blows, now conceals, now dis-
closes,
· Now it catches the gleam of the morning's
first beam,
In full glory reflected, now shines on the
stream;
'Tis the star-spangled banner! O, long may
it wave
O'er the land of the free and the home of
the brave!

And where is that band who so vaunting
    swore
That the havoc of war and battle's confusion
A home and a country should leave us no
    more?
Their blood has washed out the foul foot-
    steps' pollution.
No refuge could save the hireling and slave
From the terror of flight, or the gloom of the
    grave;
And the star-spangled banner in triumph
    doth wave
O'er the land of the free and the home of
    the brave!

O, thus be it ever when freemen shall stand,
Between their loved homes, and the war's
    desolation!
Blest with victory and peace, may the
    heaven-rescued land
Praise the power that hath made and pre-
    served us a nation!

Then conquer we must when our cause it is
just,
And this be our motto "in God is our trust,"
And the star-spangled banner in triumph
shall wave,
O'er the land of the free and the home of
the brave!

What Our Flag Says.

DON'T you see me waving here,
    Floating proudly through the air?
  I say to all beneath my fold,
    I'm dearer than rich mines of gold!
        O'er all I wave!

I won renown in seventy-nine,
    When all were filled with grief and fear;
I always waved along the front,—
    My place was never in the rear.
        I waved to win!

In more than twenty battles, then,
    I saw ten thousand sons, or more,

Give up their lives to free this soil,
And drive the Briton's from our shore,
That I might wave!

I waved o'er victory and defeat;—
They bore me safe while in retreat,—
The ground was dyed with crimson blood—
To plant me where Burgoyne stood,
That I might wave!

And when Cornwallis said that he
Would make a full surrender,
They cheered and cheered the dear old flag,
Their shouts were loud but tender;
And there I waved!

A few short years again, and I
Was called where muskets rattle,
And there twelve thousand sons, or more,
Gave up their lives in battle,
That I might wave!

Again they said, in forty-five,
That I must surely go,

And they would plant my flag-staff there,
   Way down in Mexico;
      And there I waved!

And there I saw three thousand fall,
   By the ruthless hand of war,
Which the common soldier in all lands
   With weeping does abhor.
      O'er them I waved!

And next the men that cheered me once,
   And shouted when I won,
At Sumpter rent my peaceful folds,
   And tried to shoot me down!—
      But there I waved!

They used to take me for a mask,
   So they could win renown,
And when the boys in blue approached,
   With grape they shot them down!
      O'er them I had to wave!

But I had friends, and they were true—
   They are the ones to trust;

They'll smite the hand that pulls me down,
　And trails me in the dust!
　　O'er them I'll wave!

A million men I've seen cut down,
　And many thousand more,
Beside the wounded that have died
On old Columbia's shore,
　　That I might wave!

Now all you sons give me a cheer,
　And loving daughters, too,
For Briton's flag has bowed to me,
　And the Palmetto, too.
　　O'er them I waved!

And now three cheers for the soldiers,
　The loyal, brave and true,
And I'll wave o'er those departed,
　Who fell for the red, white and blue!
　　O'er them I'll wave!

Decoration Day.

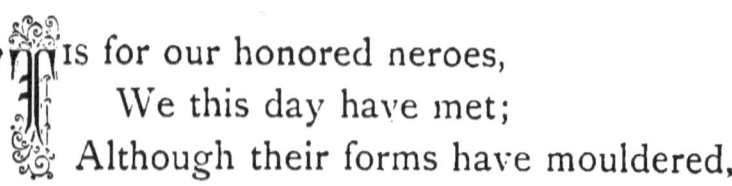

'TIS for our honored heroes,
  We this day have met;
Although their forms have mouldered,
  Their deeds we'll ne'er forget.

CHORUS—We will meet but we will miss them;
        In their homes is a vacant chair,
        And a priceless picture wrapped
        In a coil of brother's hair.

This day will bring sad memories back
  To many a broken heart;—
When the captain called his company out,
  And mother and son did part.
                        CHORUS—

We meet this day to bind anew,
  Our sacred honor and our love,
For those who fell upon the field—
  But now are in their home above.

CHORUS—

To-day our minds will backwark fly,
  To troops arrayed and passing by,
In uniforms of navy blue,
  With glittering swords all bright and new

CHORUS—

We saw them fall in prison pens,
  Their looks were ghastly wild;
But ere they crossed the vale beyond,
  They lisped the name of wife and child.

CHORUS—

We done what little we could do,
  We heard their mournful sighs,
And gently folded up their arms,
  When death had closed their eyes.

CHORUS—

Their battles are all over,
  Their toilsome march is done,
Their painful wounds are healed,—
  With them the victory's won.

CHORUS-—

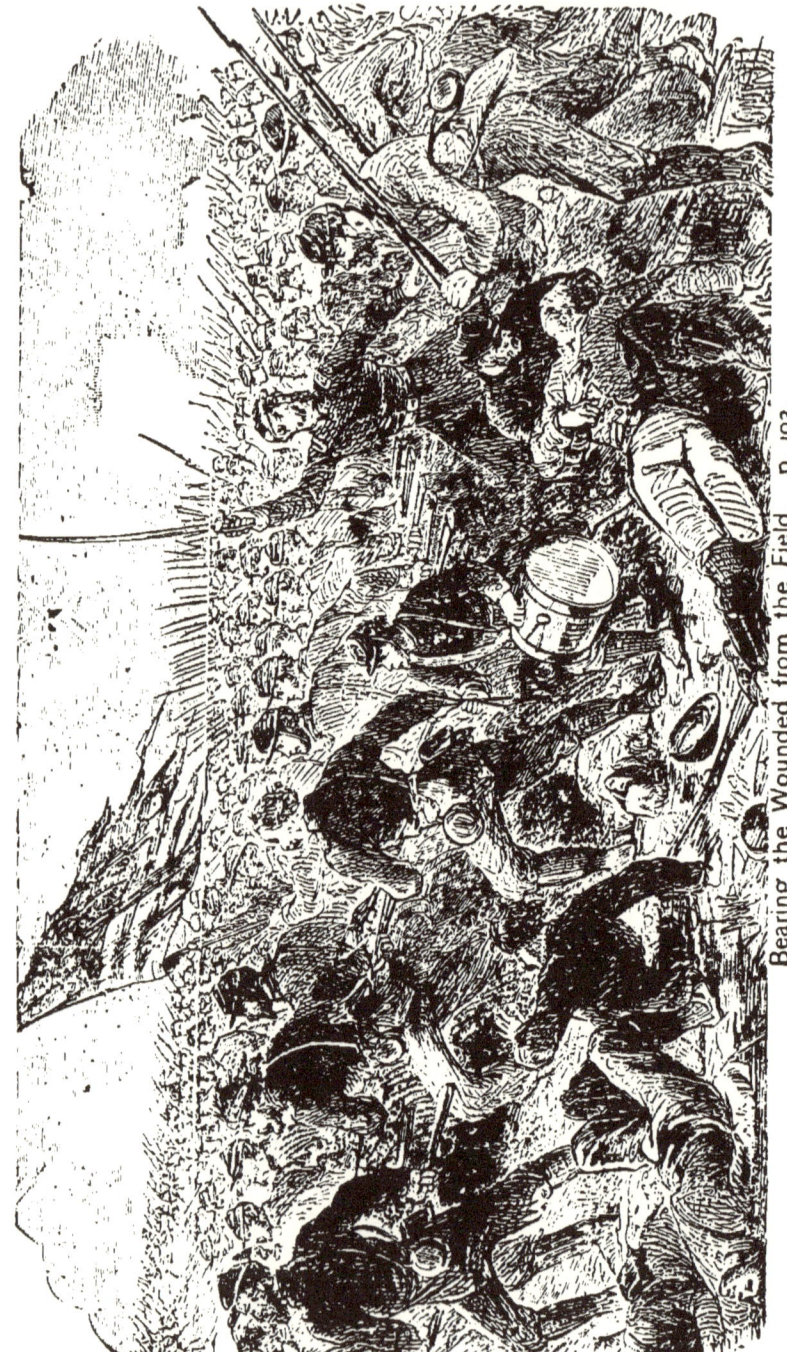

Bearing the Wounded from the Field.   p. 103.

The Dying Soldier.

E knelt beside his dying child,
   With a calm and anxious eye,
And heard him call the names at home,
   Then murmured, "I must die."

'Twas cruel lead that pierced his form,
   And tore his arm away;
The same that slew a thousand more
   Upon that summer day.

The father saw the stretcher there,
   To bear his child away;—
And then his frame it shook with grief,—
   No mortal could it stay.

He pressed his hand unto his lips,
　　And cried, "Oh! can it be,
The young, the fair, the innocent,
　　Must die for slavery?"

The groans and shrieks upon this field,
　　Under the dome of the bright blue sky,
The human forms now chilled in death,
　　Will make the bravest heave a sigh!

My country! yes, they've sung of thee!
　　But it was mockery, yes, indeed!
And now thy people they shall mourn,
　　Because thy sons are called to bleed!

My country! yes, I'm proud of thee!
　　But on thy glory was a stain;
The clanking chain and baying hound,
　　Marked out the curse on liberty's plain!

They've sung aloud of our banner bright,
　　As o'er the free it waves;
But lo! a stain was on its folds,
　　As it floated o'er millions of slaves!

And then as that father bent o'er him,
  His life-blood fast ebbing away,
In a tent away down in Georgia,
  Where the wounded and suffering lay.

A smile of remembrance passed o'er him,
  And lit up the dying one's eye,
"I'm glad, very glad of your presence;—
  But father, 'tis hard thus to die!"

Those words reached that dear father's heart,
  And all of its fountains were stirred;
His lips were palsied, no sound could he
        make,—
  In vain did he strive to utter a word!

"Now, father," said the dying son,
  His voice grew faint and low,—
"Tell mother that I send a kiss
  To her before I go.!"

His tongue was loosed, his voice returned,
  He clasped him in his last embrace:

"I will! I will!" he said,
    And pressed him to his throbbing heart,
His hero and his dead.

That marble brow with auburn hair,
    Lay lifeless on that father's breast,
Like sun-beams on the distant clouds,
    Which line the gorgeous west.

A letter, a kiss, and a coil of hair,
    That was sent to a nothern home,
And a mound of earth in Georgia's sand,
    Told what that stain had done.

Decoration Day.

W E meet this day, but some are gone.
  They who were loved as well as we;
Who left their kindred far behind,
  To shield the Tree of Liberty.

CHORUS—From east to west, from north to
      south,
    By you this land was trod;
  And now we meet and homage pay
  To our comrades under the sod.

We meet this day with mournful hearts,
  To honor those we cannot see—
Who said, by all their words and deeds:
  "Give me death or liberty!"
                    CHORUS—

We meet this day, but not as then,
   When blood like rain was running free,
O'er cloud capped hills and verdant plains,
   To save the Tree of Liberty.

                              CHORUS—

We meet, but woe is here and there,
   On many a comrade's brow we see
The well-known mark, points out the man,
   Whose cry was, "death or liberty!"

                              CHORUS—

And when we meet from year to year,
   The vacant seats of some we'll see,
Whose graves are shaded by the boughs
   Of freedom's great and stately tree.

                              CHORUS—

Our Flag.

UR flag is the pride of the nation,
'Tis dearer than diamonds or gold:
To the rich, and the boy in the cabin,
You are equal in under its fold.

CHORUS—Our glorious flag, our blood-
bought flag,
May it say to white and black:
"My golden folds shall protect you
all,—
Press forward and never turn back!"

The boy in the furrow a-plodding,
His garments are tattered, his feet are
bare:

He'll outstrip the boy in the mansion,
And sit in the President's chair.
CHORUS—

All nations had honored our ensign,
When it floated o'er bond and o'er free,
Till God in much mercy, had called one
To thrust in and cut down that great tree.
CHORUS—

Then millions on millions of voters,
Said the blacks should go forth as the
white,
Till seven at the great central D. C.
Said, "your millions of voters ain't right!"
CHORUS—

Our flag it shall float over justice,
Our voters shall join heart and hand;—
Till oppression, that dark visaged monster,
Like the dew shall be swept from our land.
CHORUS—

Our flag is the pride of our seamen,
  When in mart or in main 'tis unfurled,
Like a cable that cannot be broken,
  Binds commerce all over the world.

CHORUS—

Decoration Day.

———◦◦◦⊰⊱◦◦◦———

'TWAS for our nation, yes indeed,
　That those we mourn were called to
　　　bleed;
　'Twas for our nation, that the brave,
　　Were called to fill a soldier's grave.

CHORUS—Yes, you said you loved your free-
　　　dom;
　　With your blood your words
　　　were sealed!
　That our nation then nor never,
　　We to traitorous sons would
　　　yield!

We see them now, as we saw them then;
  They marched with us, fought side by
    side,
While we were spared to tell the tale;
  Their blood it flowed a crimson tide.

CHORUS—

We marched with them o'er mountain tops,
  And hillside slopes so long,
And heard them sing, while tramping through
  Some patriotic song.

CHORUS—

And through the din of battle,
  We saw the stretcher there
To bear away our comrades,
  Whose groanings filled the air.

CHORUS—

Through tangled swamps, and swollen
    streams,
  Our fallen comrades trod;
Till by the ruthless hand of war,
  They sleep beneath the sod.

And, now, dear comrades, ere we part,
  We'll pledge ourselves, that we
Will meet each year and homage pay,
  To those who fill our national cemet'ry.

CHORUS—

No More Pensions.

WHO are crying no more pension's?
  'Tis not the true and loyal ones;—
'Tis not the blood that drenched our
    country—
  Saved us from that awful doom!

Who are crying no more pension's?
  'Tis not the sons beneath the clay,
They who saved our country for us,
  Preserved what we enjoy to-day.

Who are crying no more pensions?
  'Tis not the mothers through our land,
Who are mourning for their loved ones,
  Lying in the southern sand.

Who are crying no more pensions?
　'Tis not the boys who can't be seen,
Who rotted in some southern prison
　With scurvy and the foul gangreen.

Who are crying no more pensions?
　'Tis not those whom Winder slew,
Nor those who fell by a rebel battery,
　Masked to catch the boys in blue.

What is crying no more pensions? ·
　'Taint wooden legs and patent arms;
Eyes which you can touch and handle,
　But ne'er can see earth's glorious charms.

What made the Year 1865 Memorable.

HE year 1865 was made memorable in the annals of history, as being the one in which the so-called confederate leaders laid down the arms they had taken from this nation to wage war against it. From the hour that gray headed seer fired the first gun in Fort Sumpter in April, '61, our country was one continual scene of strife and bloody battles. At the north fathers, mothers, brothers and sisters wept burning tears when they were called to part with loved ones, to go they knew not where. Perhaps to the wilds of Kentucky, Tennessee, or the burning sands of the south, to fall upon the battle-field, languish in some prison, or fall a prey to disease! The thought of all this caused mothers to weep as no one else can weep. Upon the battle-field was suffering so intense, no mortal tongue can ever depict the agonies. Men have sought out many inventions, but that is something mortal man can never do. They can not picture out a battle-field in anyway so those who did not participate can have even a faint idea of its horrifying looks. We will stop for one moment, and consider a field where men are lying dead in heaps like sheaves upon a harvest field. Upon one field ten thousand dead, twenty thousand wounded, many of them in contortions, groaning and struggling in the agonies of death; every foot of ground covered with some missile of death and crimsoned with the blood of the wounded. They were suffering untold agonies, dying, that our nation might not become a by-word among the nations of the earth, as a star that had shone with exceeding brightness and then disappeared, leaving a spot blacker than Egyptian darkness, such were the scenes upon the battle-field; while in homes far away the anxious mother was hourly watching the latest casualities to learn the whereabouts of her loved ones, and with throbbing heart and tearful eyes, and sorrow such as none can tell, she read the long lists of dead, wounded, prisoners and missing, to catch a familiar name, only to add to her already appalling grief. The year 1865 saw great changes. The last battles were fought and a long and bloody rebellion crushed. The armies of the West joined the armies of the East, and in the shadow of the nation's Capitol marched down Pennsylvania Avenue and saluted the Chief Magistrate of the Republic as the representative of the civil power of the nation. It was said by some at home that the army could never be disbanded without general destruction everywhere.

That the soldiers had become so accustomed to pillaging, they would plunder and murder regardless of law. But we all know this proved false, the men who had by their courage, suffering and sacrifices, saved the country, at the first moment their services were not needed, saluted the old flag, which they had followed so long, and to which they had given new glory. Dropped musket and saber, cartridge-box and knapsack and hurried home to father, mother, wife, brother and sister. They were returning home in squads on different trains to all parts of the country; officers were giving touching farewells to their commands, rendering tributes of praise to the brave defenders of our nation, for all the noble deeds they had done and the untold sacrifices they had made. They expressed the deepest sorrow for the bereaved friends of the lamented dead, who had fallen on the battle-field, in prisons, hospitals, in camp, or on the march, by disease far from home, and the consola-

tion and assistance of near and dear friends.
The work which they enlisted to perform
had been well done. Those returning home
were the ones whom foul disease had spared
and the deadly bullets of many battles
had missed. They went to their homes with
the proud assurance of having participated
in many hard fought battles. They went to
their homes as American citizens, knowing
what it had cost to maintain our national
integrity. They asked nothing for themselves, neither bounty, office or immunity.
They asked only that they might go back to
their homes, and commence anew the battle
of life, and endeavor to make good the losses
incurred by their absence. So they returned,
but not to find things as they left them.
They went home to find the farm wasted
and frequently encumbered by reason of ex-
penses, that out-ran the soldier's small in-
come. Business had taken to itself wings;
a new hand at the bench, at the forge, in the
shop, behind the counter, in the office, and

in thousands of cases the place that once knew them, would know them no more, forever!

The service which united the country and made it powerful and prosperous, diminished the wealth and added to the poverty of those who, under providence, had wrought it all. Yet they did not complain, nor do they now. The country they saved they have not reproached; the union soldier did not fight for mere pay, or after reward. His reward is not in houses nor lands. It is in the priceless treasure of memory. In the proud consciousness of duty done even at the peril of life. He does not own so much which he can specifically call his own, and reduce to possession as he might have done had he not enlisted and served in the army. But his undivided portion of the great whole is larger. He can look abroad over the vast domain that his blood and suffering helped cement together, and see the treasure wrested from the soil he helped to redeem. He can see the wonderful inventions and all of the evidences of a prosperous and diligent people. He can lay his hand on his heart and trustfully say of all this, "I am an integral part. I am an American citizen. If I had not by my blood and service, helped cement together the union, instead of the peaceful fields in which the husbandman can safely labor from the rising of the sun to the going down thereof, these would have been divided and waring states, ruin would have reigned supreme, where peace and prosperity now abound. The American people would have learned no art but war!" So long as the love of a country shall survive among the generations of the American people, or liberty make her home under the protection of the republic, the example of the soldier's patriotic devotion will not die for lack of honorable remembrance or worthy imitation.

Many of the noblest, bravest and best who went out did not return. They left them on the hillsides, in the valleys and by the

streams of the south, where no voice of
mother, sister or wife will ever awaken them,
where no kind frinds will strew flowers upon their graves, but they will never be for-
gotten. Their heroic deeds and last resting
place will always be remembered by their
comrades, while their looks will remain
bright in the memory of relatives and friends,
though dead they will live in the affections
of their countrymen, and their country's
history. The friendship formed in bivouac
and on the battle-field, will never be forgot-
ten, whether in the same regiment, brigade
or division, the friendship of the war was
strong.

While we are enjoying cheerful surround-
ings, let us not fail to remember those who
have gone before, who sealed their devotion
with their blood, and who now sleep in the
soil they died to make free. The vanished
and nameless army of the republic, who
were not merely willing to die but to be for-
gotten; that the good they did might live after

them; what they died to preserve we enjoy to-day. The ranks of the soldiers are getting thinner, but the lessons they teach should, and will be, deeply impressed upon the mind of the rising generation, in whose hearing all will be recounted; the lesson bequeathed from father to son will not be lost. Its admonitions will prevent future rebellions by keeping alive that spirit of patriotism which finds expression in national unity in equal and exact justice to all men.   In complete obedience to the will of the majority, and in the equal enforcement of all laws.

In conclusion, our government should see that no one who faithfully served his country in the hour of its peril should die in want.

Welcome of 1865.

THERE was shouting in the mansion,
    In the lowly cabin, too,
When the hosts of dark rebellion
    Said, "we'll fight no more with you—
        We'll surrender!"

Welcome, welcome, was the greeting!
    From hearts at home it quickly came;
The words were caught, and all repeating
    "Come, Oh! come!
        Welcome home!"

You have saved our nation for us,
    By your blood and suffering, too,

Welcoming the Return of Soldiers in 1865.

From the men who tried to crush us,
  They who filled our land with woe.
      Welcome home!

Where are they who mustered with you?
  Fought the bloody battles through!
They whose deeds will ne'er be spoken,
  They who filled the prisons, too!
      Oh! where are they?

They were wounded, killed and lost,
  They were starved by cruel hands!
All the news we bring of some,
  They lie beneath the southern sands—
      Our comrades dear!

From the weary march and bivouac,
  From battle-fields so fierce and gory,
All are in our hearts to-day,
  Sacred ever, more in story.
      Welcome home!

At Fort Donaldson you waited
  For the fleet upon the river,

Then with dead you filled the gulches,
  Tennesseeans to deliver.
    Welcome home!

Welcome, welcome! We remember
  Of the noted Nashville route,
Then with pointed steel you ever
  Made the rebels face about.
    Welcome home!

Welcome, welcome home! From Franklin,
  By your courage—death defying—
While your comrades low were lying,
  Back you sent the rebels flying!
    Welcome home!

Then you saw the rebel host;—
  Officers with faces solemn,
Infantry in flying column,
  Enough of war to fill a volume,
    Welcome home!

At Chickamauga, Pittsburg and Antietam,
  Pea-Ridge and South Mountain gorges,

The Wilderness, Fair Oaks
And Gettysburg—the theme enlarges
Welcome home!

Welcome, welcome! How you cheered!
When you heard that Vicksburg's taken!
With cannon, roar, and deafening shout,
The very ground beneath was shaken.
Welcome home!

Welcome, welcome home from Corinth,
Where hand to hand, you fought the foe;
Stumbling o'er the dead and wounded,
Until thousands were laid low.
Welcome home!

Welcome, welcome! what a darkness
Hovered o'er us one and all,
When brave Thomas seemed o'erpowered,
And his strength about to fall!
Welcome home!

When you heard the shout of Logan,
Calling to avenge the blood

Of your loved and brave McPherson,
  Who had like a fortress stood.
    Welcome home!

Welcome, welcome! then you answered,
  Put this vile rebellion down!
Dig the poisonous upas up,
  Ere the tree is larger grown!
    Welcome home!

Welcome, welcome! you the gallant Hood
    surrounded,
  And the prized Atlanta won;
Quickly through the north it sounded,
  The good work that you had done.
    Welcome home!

For that battle ask of Sherman,
  What's the glory?
He will answer, "home elysian,
  Robes of ermine you should wear!"
    Welcome home!

Welcome, welcome from Fort Fisher,
  You their giant ramparts battered,

Till the fort was badly shattered,
  And the flag of treason tattered!
    Welcome home!

In the face of bristling cannon,
  Grape and musketry,
When your bleeding ranks were thinning
  On you rushed to crush the gray.
    Welcome home!

One by one you took each traverse;
  At Fort Anderson you halted,
Then over its intrenchments vaulted,
  And won the works you had assaulted.
    Welcome home!

Then cheer on cheer went up from all,
  In one unbroken, deafening shout,
When you saw the stars and stripes
  Float proudly from that bold redoubt!
    Welcome home!

Welcome, welcome!   We are thinking,
  Of that long and bloody route,

When brave Sheridan just returning—
Made the rebels face about.
Welcome home!

Then you saw the flying columns,
Of the rebs all clad in gray;
Then you cheered and cheered for Sheridan,
Who heard you twenty miles away.
Welcome home!

From Kenesaw and Rocky Face,
Up the valley, down the coast,
You have conquered, won the glory;—
You the patriotic host,
Welcome home!

Welcome, welcome! Those were battles,
Which the world is proud to name;
Freeing all the human chattels,
Filling traitorous hearts with shame.
Welcome home!

Welcome. welcome for those battles—ask
Ulysses,

What of honor you may know,
He will answer, "home elysian,
More than mortals can bestow!"
Welcome home!

Welcome, welcome! We have shrined you
In the temple of our hearts,
With a golden cord entwined you,
That no foe can thrust apart.
Welcome home!

Welcome, welcome! God has kept you,
All those weary days agone;
Though of comrades he bereft you,
He but gathered in his own.
Welcome home!

'Tis for the sleeping heroes
In their distant graves,
We the silent tears are weeping,
While their blood-bought banner waves.
Welcome home!

'Twas saved by you in battles gory,
  Now its sacred folds can never
Traitors dare presume to sever,
  Lo! it waves now and forever.
    Welcome home!

Decoration Day.

S LEEP, comrades, sleep!
 We are watching o'er your clay,
Thinking of the trying scenes
  When from home you marched away
  At your country's call

Sleep, comrades, sleep.
 Of the days we now are thinking,
When with us you all unshrinking
  Thought to weld the chain, unlinking,
  Through our native land.

Sleep, comrades, sleep!
 'Tis the toilsome march we view,
When with gun and knapsack, too,

Many miles we marched with you,
    Weary and worn.

Sleep, comrades, sleep!
'Tis the foe we now behold
Rushing onward for the fray!
    As they come in days of old,
        Clad in somber robes of gray

Sleep, comrades, sleep!
    Now we hear the cannon's roar!
Now we see the deadly charge,
    As we did in days of yore,
        When our land was drenched with gore!

Sleep, comrades, sleep;
    Now we see the panting steed,
Bear his gallant rider where
    Naught but death could claim a part,
        Where deadly missiles filled the air!

Sleep, comrades, sleep!
    To save our country dear,

We saw your bleeding form,
  Mangled and torn by storms
    Of solid shot and shell!

Sleep, comrades, sleep!
  When the smoke had passed away,
And darkness stilled the battle's fray,
  Then we placed your lifeless clay,
    Beneath the valley's sod.

Sleep, comrades, sleep!
  A few short years this earth we'll trod,
Then we will enter through,
  At his command, pass under the rod,
    And be welcomed there by you!

Ode.

—————·∞·❀·∞·—————

W E come, we come, a loyal band,
    As children of this nation,
We'll join in heart, we'll join in hand,
    To keep the declaration.

From east to west, from north to south,
    We're filled with exultation!
Our honored dead reminds us now,
    To keep the declaration!

The soldiers in the battles, fierce,
    Afighting for this nation,
Gave up their homes, their lives, their all,
    To save the declaration!

And when we know this day was won
  By blood and tribulation,
The stars and stripes that urged them on
  Will swell the declaration!

And when we meet beside their graves,
  For sacred consecration,
Though they are dead, their deeds will say,
  Just keep the declaration!

We'll not forget that sacred bell,
  That pealed with exultation,
To tell the wan and weary ones,
  About the declaration.

And as the years do swiftly fly,
  And freedom's birthday draweth nigh,
We'll raise the anthem to the sky,
  And hail the declaration!

And when that glorious day does dawn
  We'll welcome it at rise of sun,
With shouts of joy and muffled drum,
  And through the day we'll meet as one,
    And read the declaration!

Pensions all Paid.

—∘∘◦❀◦∘∘—

In behalf of the ex-union soldiers whose names appear every week in newspaper columns, complaining because they cannot get their pensions, those who to-day are infirm and tottering upon the verge of the grave, without the necessities of life, those who contracted diseases while in the army, and upon their return home would not ask for a pension, and at last are separated from officers and comrades, and are unable to find any of their company or regiment to aid them in obtaining a pension; those whom years ago the nation was proud of, their deeds of bravery were heralded from the hills of Maine to the peaceful waters of the

Pacific, from the British possessions to the gulf; when they marched to the defense of our country they were in the prime of life, their step was then firm and elastic, and their forms erect, now their step is slow and their forms are bowed with disease, hardship, care and old age, their eyes that used to flash at the sounding of the charge are now dim, their raven locks are now streaked with gray, and they will soon join their comrades who fell upon the bloody fields of battle, whose bones lie beneath the soil they died to protect; in behalf of those I insert the following lines:

OLDIERS they have had their pensions,
    Drew them twenty years ago,
Drew them when they saved our country
    From a bold and deadly foe.

Soldiers they have drew their pensions,
    Drew them in the battle's din; —

Drew them when they starved and languished
    In some southern prison pen.

Soldiers they have had their pensions,
    Drawn when death was raging high;
Where the dust and smoke of battle,
    Rose and hid the bright blue sky.

Soldiers they have had their pensions,
    Paid with shot and leaden balls,
Bacon brown and hard-tack tough,
    When the chilling torrent falls.

Soldiers they have had their pensions,
    Money cannot them repay;
Some have homesteads six by four,—
    Sacred graves in southern clay.

Soldiers they have had their pensions,
    Paid in prison, camp and line;
Paid with hunger woe and death,
    Borne with fortitude divine.

Soldiers they have had their pensions,
    Paid with English shot and shell,

Paid with murder, wounds and groans,
　　Where our brave defenders fell.

Soldiers they should have their pensions,
　　From the nation they have saved,
For the years they spent in battle,
　　For the horrors they have braved.

Can our blood-bought land forget
　　Its defenders, brave and dear,
Has our sun of justice set?
　　Is our night of justice near?

Decoration Day.

REST, comrades, rest!
　　Now we stand beside your graves,
For your march on earth is o'er;
　　No more you'll hear the sentry's call
Upon this changing shore.

CHORUS—For you we're strewing flowers,
　　　　Beautiful flowers of May,
　　O'er the graves of our fallen comrades,
　　　　Whose forms have mouldered to
　　　　　　clay.

　　Rest, comrades, rest!
You were the nation's loyal sons,
You were the true and brave!

Nobly you fought beneath our flag,
  Our nation, dear to save!
                    Chorus—

  Rest, comrades, rest!
You fought, and bled, and died;—
  You did not return from the war,
But our hearts through life will yearn
  For the boys who will come never more.
                    Chorus—

  Rest, comrades, rest!
Some fell by the way while a marching,
  And thousands were shot through the heart
And thousands from dark rebel prisons
  From comrades were called to depart.
                    Chorus—

  Rest, comrades, rest!
No more you'll hear the cannon's roar,
  Nor the drum's redoubling beat,
Nor the order given for a deadly charge,
  Nor join in a wild retreat.
                    Chorus—

Rest, comrades, rest!
We know that our comrades are happy;
    They were faithful to country and God,
But their names and their deeds will grow
        brighter,
    Of our comrades under the sod.

                        CHORUS—

Rest, comrades, rest!
They rest, but that curse it is ended,
    And the dark sons of Africa are free;
They rest, but that glorious emblem
    Proudly floats o'er the land of the free!

                        CHORUS—

Rest, comrades, rest!
What you died to preserve we enjoy,
    Though no marble may mark out the spot,
Yet the place where you fell for our
        country,
    By the nation will ne'er be forgot.

                        CHORUS—

Oh! the Dead Were There!

AWAY in the far sunny southland,
   Were forms surpassing fair,
Encased in walls of ponderous size,—
   But Oh! the dead were there!

CHORUS—What bound them in those pens so
            vile,
      The loyal sons of America,—
      They who were true as Washing-
            ton?
      'Twas accursed slavery!

There were kind and loving fathers,
   A breaking in despair;

The tired and noble forms of youth
  Were daily dying there.

CHORUS—

While all around beneath our flag,
  Was grain and viands rare,
And within those rugged walls
  The brave were starving there!

CHORUS—

All hopes were crushed within their breast;
  'Twas banishment and care,
To hear the dying beg for bread,
  And know the dead were there!

CHORUS—

Outside 'twas mirth and the wine cup;
  Within, a current of despair!
For the hardened sons of earth
  Cared not for the dead in there.

CHORUS—

But they'll shudder, start and tremble!
They'll wail in deep despair,
When they hear the words, "depart!
For those you slew in there!"

CHORUS-

Just Twenty Years Ago.

———◦◦◇◦◇◦◦———

HAT was that I heard you say?
  Mother, did you call, or no?
Yes, my son, for I've been˚ thinking
  Of just twenty years ago.

CHORUS—Think of all the sighs and tears,
          Think of all the grief and woe,
        That was in a million homes
          Just twenty years ago.

That hour shines brighter now, to-night,
  That hour of vital grief and woe,
Than when I read that solemn message
  Just twenty years ago.

                        CHORUS—

Guard of Honor escorting Gen. Sickles from the battle field of Gettysburg.

Yes, you wrote that Frank had fallen,
  While bravely charging on the foe;
'Twas here, I read that trying message
  Just twenty years ago.

CHORUS—

When I recall that day and hour,
  Tears will unbidden flow,
For one who passed from earth away
  Just twenty years ago.

CHORUS—

And while my days are lengthened out,
  And years do onward flow,
Sad memory will recall the scene
  Of twenty years ago.

CHORUS—

And when I've crossed that valley o'er,
  That's free from earthly grief and woe,
Then I shall see the one that fell
  Just twenty years ago.

CHORUS—

PART III.

TEMPERANCE.

A Plea to Voters.

—————◦◦◦◦◦◦◦◦◦—————

OME all you noble voters,
   I pray you lend an ear;
   Let's have more food and clothing,
   And less of rum and beer.

The brewers they have heaped their cash;
   The pile looms up each year,
But the wife and children have been robbed,
   By their sale of rum and beer.

They say their business is upright!
   But that sounds very queer,
For count the graves untimely filled
   By their sale of rum and beer.

And must the brewers rule the vote,
  Of our blood-bought country dear;
While weeping mothers see their sons
  Cast down by rum and beer?

There's many questions that are great
  But they must take the rear,
For the vital one, to save our land
  Is to crush old rum and beer.

The cry goes up on every hand,
  Let the tippler have his dram;
Let him drink and run his course
  As quickly as he can!

If he was the one that suffered all,
  And not his children dear,
The curse would not be half so great,
  That is caused by rum and beer.

We see a solid wall of shops filled
  With a tempting bait,
Yet brewer's say 'tis not a crime
  To tempt a man to sin.

And yet two hundred drunkards
  Die each day.
Without a sigh from the men who slew,
  They're quickly tumbled in.

Men are crying, regulate, regulate the law!
  Why don't you regulate a well-known
    ague chill,
The only way to deal with both,
  Just use a sure and certain pill.

For years they tried to compromise,
  And regulate the law,
But then as now, there was a curse,
  A great and crushing flaw.

Till Abram took his pen and said,
  "No more you'll see
Our glorious flag a-floating o'er,
  The bondman and the free!"

If there's any truth or justice,
  Hovering o'er this hemisphere,
Shield the wan and weeping mothers,
  That are crushed by rum and beer.

The brewers chuckle in their sleeves,
   When election day draws near,
Thinking of the votes they'll win
   That will favor rum and beer.

And shall we have on our banner,
   Free whisky and free trade—
And let the weeping mothers mourn
   O'er the now protection raid?

If the sufferers can't get justice,
   By the men that vote each year,
Let the ones that rock the cradle
   Crush out old rum and beer!

Temperance.

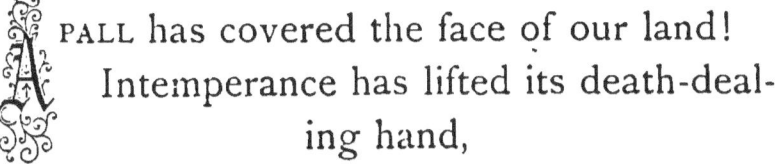

A PALL has covered the face of our land!
Intemperance has lifted its death-deal-
ing hand,
And the darkness of liquor is witnessed
and felt,
For whisky has deluged our country
with guilt.

But a star has risen so dazzling bright,
It says to our voters, prepare for the fight!
Stand firm by your colors, your helmet
must be,
To say by your votes you'll trample whisky!

It has reveled in wealth, been sumptuously
fed,

It has robbed the poor wife of her clothing
    and bread,
It has tempted the young and the weak
    passer by,
Made demons of them in the gutter to lie.

It takes the money and brains of our men;
The fruits of that monster lie in some barred
    pen;
'Tis foremost in vice and dens of low fame,
Its face is of brass, and whisky's its name.

It builds up saloons and the keepers get rich,
While the men it has robbed are cast in
    some ditch;
But what do they care? for they want the
    last bill.
They will rob your dear children their pock-
    ets to fill!

And there is the druggist so wonderful wise,
He'll fix up a foam that will dazzle your
    eyes;

"It Builds up Saloons, and the Keepers get Rich, While the Men it has Robbed are Cast in Some Ditch." p. 160.

But in a dark corner he'll sell you the same,
Something he's ashamed of, and whisky's its
name!

There are some of our doctors—I'll mention
no name,—
They in the dark, will sell you the same;
They'll put in some bark from the wild
cherry tree,
And say it was medicine for the whole
family.

But the star of bright temperance shall
whisky outshine,
As gold from the mint does the dross from
the mine.
It has rose like a beacon light, streaming
afar;
Oh! welcome! thrice welcome! bright
temperance star!

Thy brightness shall guide the inebriate's
hope,

And teach him in strength with old whisky
    to cope.
To thee shall the woe-stricken look and
    rejoice.
To thee lift in gratitude many a voice.

Thou hast risen in beauty, Oh! never to
    fade.
Beneath thee, our voters are proudly dis-
    played.
With thee as our champion they'll vanquish
    the foe,
And look o'er a land that is purged from
    its woe.

Dialogue.

"Good morning, Charlie!"
"Good morning, Fred. Got a new rig.
haven't you?"

"Yes; I took this out of old Miller."

"You don't mean to say you stole that
from Miller, do you?"

"O, no! I just took it from him."

"You are talking Chinese now, Charle.
You will have to send for an intetperter."

"Well, Fred, I will be my own interperter.
You see I joined the temperance league six

months ago, and this is the result. If I had kept on traveling the same road I have traveled for six years, old Miller would have had this carriage, that beautiful bay horse, harness and all, cramed down into his pocket; or had it in that palatial residence he is building on Pearl street. I'll just tell you, Fred, what's a fact: Old Miller has pocketed the last cent of my father's hard earnings that he ever will!"

"Charlie, did you hear what a smash up they had down to O——— last week?"

"No; since Miller and I dissolved, I find plenty of employment without going to O—— to get the daily mail."

"Charlie, I suppose you will listen if I relate the tale?"

"Certainly, certainly, Fred!"

"Last Thursday, about a dozen got into a fight at Miller's. Some got terribly smashed up; there was no respect shown to officers, or privates, the marshal getting several welts on and about the head. Deacon Jones'

son, Will, got drunk and spent all his money;
then Miller turned him out and told him to
go home. You know it was a terrible cold
night; he was found about half a mile from
town in the ditch by the road-side, nearly
frozen to death. It came very near killing
his mother. Old Jake Stevens had been
there four days, drunk all the time; when he
went home after the battle, his wife told him
she had not had anything for herself and
children to eat since the day before, while
he was down to Old Miller's, spending
money enough to have kept them all winter;
told him he had drawn the money for building Miser's house, and now it was all gone,
she wanted to get the children some clothing
and shoes, so they could go to school; said
she could never send them to school like
other children, because all the clothes they
had she had to wash for, and buy them. Then
Stevens raved to the highest pitch, grabbed
a club and knocked the brains out of two,
and would have killed more, but Baily hap-

pened along, heard the racket, got a rope
and tied Stevens. He'll stretch hemp, now,
and everybody will be glad, I guess. I
should think his wife and children would
want them to hurry up the execution. He'll
have just one mourner, and that will be Old
Miller. He'll shed crocodile tears, I expect, thinking about the money he would
have if Stevens had pulled through a few
years longer!"

"Come, Fred, just say that you will never
touch another drop!"

"Charlie, when I see what you have saved
by your reformation, I am tempted to say
I'll touch not, taste not! But what will my
old chums say? They will hoot at me, call
me a baby, stingy, and so on!"

"What do you care for that? It will only
be for a short time. Hold up your head and
tell them you have made up your mind that
you might as well have a little loose change
in time of need, as for Miller to have it all.
I can point you to fifty men that spend near-

ly every cent they make at Miller's! What does he care for them? Not half as much as he does for his dog. All he wants is their money, and then he will kick them out and laugh in his sleeve because they are such fools to rob their families, nearly starve their wives and children. There's Bill Dingman's family; I'll bet they haven't had any shoes on their feet yet this winter!"

"Charlie, you have convinced me. I see plainly it is one of the most debasing vices that mortal man ever indulged in, and from now, henceforth and forever, I'll drink no more. We'll shake hands on that!"

Moderate Drinking.

S moderate drinking is the great high-
way,
By which all drunkard's pass.

CHORUS—Come, and sign the pledge with
me,
For whisky now it is too free!
Will you go, will you go?
If you'll say it is a sin,
The train will stop and take you in;
Will you go, will you go?

If you'll shun that dangerous route
There will be no wrecks about.
CHORUS—

That broad highway is for the stage,
So come and take the narrow gague!

CHORUS—

Now mount the train and don't look back,
And it will never fly the track.

CHORUS—

'Twill leave the tempter in the rear,
And shun old rum and lager beer.

CHORUS—

Supremely blind must tipplers be,
Though here and there a track they see.

CHORUS—

Make up your mind that you will turn,
Ere death shall pack you in his urn!

CHORUS—

Now do cease tampering with the foe,
Nor in the way of ruin go.

CHORUS—

Come, give your pledge and do abstain:
Embrace the cause and safe remain.

CHORUS—

Temperance.

———◦◦◦✥◦◦◦———

AKE room for the thousands on thousands returning
From the lowly pathway of darkness!
Our hearts with accents of kindness are
yearning;—
Unfurl your proud banner and welcome them in!

From the isles of the ocean, the plains and
the dells,
Thousands on thousands are watching the
stream;
The fond mother's heart in gratitude swells—
Oh! say, shall we wake and find this a
dream?

O'er cities and towns, o'er valleys and
    mountains,
  May the flag of temperance o'er all be
      unfurled!
It bids you partake of the life-giving foun-
      tain,—
  Those waters are flowing to gladden the
      world!

Oh! still at our post we stand to deliver,
  Till the light burns again on each deso-
      late hearth,
And the demon of whisky is vanquished for-
      ever,
  Whose breath like a plague has darkened
      the earth!

Sign the Pledge.

HERE is the man who would not shrink
From the bondage of strong drink?

CHORUS—Cheerily, readily, come along,
        Sign our pledge and sing our
        song!

If you'll only make the start,
You will act the wiser part!
                CHORUS—

Where's the man his bottle tips?—
He's in danger who but sips!
                CHORUS—

Come, then, Charlie, Fred and Lew
The temperance cause is gaining, too!

CHORUS—

Say to your friends, where ere they be,
Come and sign the pledge with me.

CHORUS—

'Tis rum that makes me fierce and wild,
'Tis rum that robs my wife and child.

CHORUS—

It robs the pocket, racks the brain,
From the maddning drink I will refrain!

CHORUS—

And when you make your New Year's call
Just say you do not drink at all.

CHORUS—

Say to the girls, where ere they be,
"That very drink may ruin me!"

CHORUS—

PART IV.

MISCELLANEOUS.

The Tree of Liberty.

———•••👯○○•———

WE meet this day, this sacred hour,
To bind anew our country's power;
From north to south, from shore to shore,
To talk of scenes in days of yore.

CHORUS—Our blood-bought country thee,
Oh! may thy soil protected be!
And shaded by the stately boughs,
Of freedom's great and glorious
tree!
Land where our fathers bled!—
Land of our kindred dead!—
By them this light was shed—
The light of liberty!

We fancy we can see the boat,
  That bore our fathers o'er!
Our liberty was cradled there;
  Old ocean wafted it ashore.

Our fathers bore the cruel laws,
  That British Lords have always made,
Till liberty was there inscribed,
  And in the silent grave was laid.

They raised the coffin from the tomb,
  And vowed to plant that precious boon,
O'er all the land from sea to sea—
  That glorious tree of liberty!

At Lexington was the first scene,
  Where blood was poured upon the green;
That blood was pure and it ran free,
  To save the tree of liberty!

At Bunker Hill again we see,
  A crimson current drench that tree;
They gained the victory—ah! how well—
  And marked the spot where Warren fell.

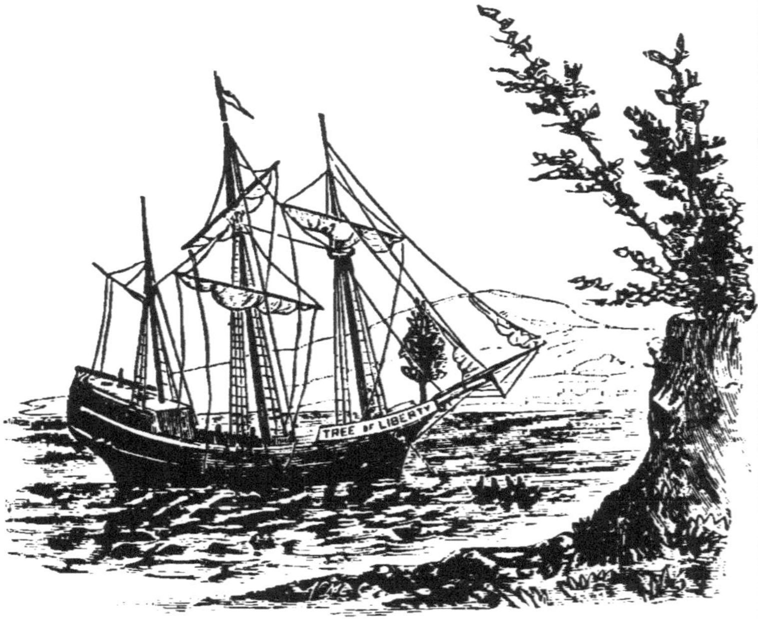
TREE of LIBERTY

The Mayflower, in whose Cabin the first written form of Government was ever Subscribed by a whole people. Hence the Birth Place of our American Liberty, rocked on the free waves of the mighty Atlantic.

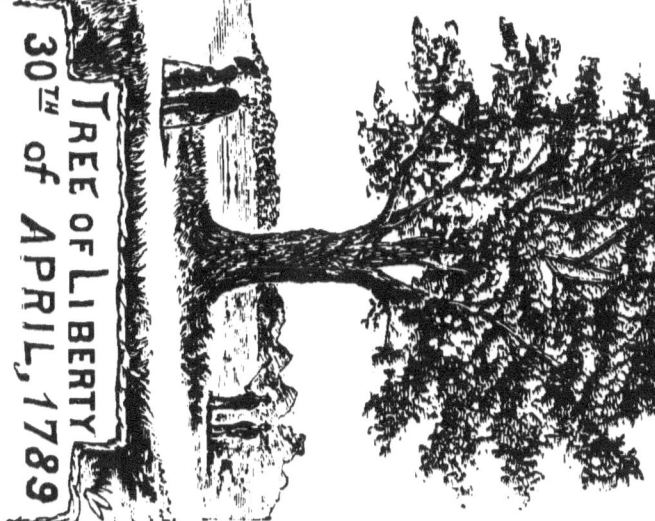

TREE OF LIBERTY
30TH of APRIL, 1789

Our fathers bore the deepest woe,
Through burning sun and drifting snow;
They fought for seven long years, that we
Might have this glorious liberty.

And while the years do roll their round,
Oh, may Columbia's sons be found
To guard the branches of that tree,
By shouting death or liberty.

And may they shield our ensign, too,
'Twas borne aloft the battles through;
It floats so proudly to the breeze,
The champion of all lands and seas!

From east to west, from north to south,
As each returning Fourth we see,
We'll shout the anthem through the land.
Our fathers died to plant that tree!

That glorious tree protected will stand
Perfuming the earth and the sky;
The joy of the true, and the pride of our land,
And shade us the Fourth of July.

They are Passing Away.

They are passing away, those fleeting
        years,
  Like leaves on the river cast,
    They wait not for man, but onward they
        flow;
    Seconds, minutes, hours, days, weeks,
        months, they go
    Into the wonderful past.

They are gliding past like a weaver's thread,
  And straight as the lightning's pointed
        gleam,
And soft as the gentle summer's breeze,
That lightly sways the forest trees,
  And daintly ripples the glassy stream.

They are gliding past, like the thistles down,
  And still as the midnight dream,
And pure as the lark, when she tunes her
    throat
To sing in the woodland her sweetest note;
  Those fleeting years so tender they seem.

Yes, they are passing, one by one,
  Down the steps of time so rare;
We stop and think of their noiseless tread,
Of the centuries past, and long since dead,
  That were beautiful and fair.

Our years are few, though to some are given
  Their three score years and ten;
But that is a short and toilsome stay,
  For the fallen sons of men.
So rapid they fly from mortals below,
As swift as an arrow from the archer's bow;
  Bear each one onward through bliss and
    woe.

As our years are few and fleeting, too,
  Shall we pass them in idle strife?

Shall we trample them under our busy feet—
Those beautiful years, so precious and
sweet—
As we travel the pathway of life?

And while our years are lengthened out,
Harsh words should not be heard;
But our life be a pattern of rare design.
Until we are called this clay to resign,
We should speak no evil word.

Lamentation.

HARK! what mournful sounds we hear,
  From mother, wife and sister dear!
The wounds grow worse from year to
    year,
  And can't be healed.

A wife, she lisped the name of one
  She deeply mourned, and dearly loved;
Whose footsteps she would hear no more,
  Whose spirit was in heaven above.

And loving sisters, when they meet,
  And see the vacant chairs of two,
Whose looks are bright as when they left—
  'Twas brother John and Lew!

The grass grows green above their graves,
  Each year its freshnes will unfold—
And this is why loved ones lament,
  For grief so deep will ne'er grow old.

The winds will waft their fragrance by,
  But to hearts bereft by a cruel war,
Sad, sad are the mem'ries they will waft,
  As we think of the fields of human gore.

Yes, we heard a mother call,
  'Twas in her silent midnight dream,
For four whose forms had turned to dust,
  Beside the onward rushing stream.

Some one had died; they wondered why!
  The bell had tolled just forty-three,
Oh! why should death claim such a one,
  Beloved by all, and young as she!

But some one heard her call the names
  Of four she mourned and dearly loved;
Then wonder why that mother fled,
  And soared to rest with them above.

Reflection.

E are traveling, we are traveling,
   Traveling through this vale of tears,
To that undiscovered country,
   Where there is no end of years.

We are looking, we are looking,
   O'er a land by millions trod;
Thinking of the generations
   That have mouldered 'neath the sod.

We are standing, we are standing,
   On a land to mortals given;
But ere men have learned to live,
   The clay and spirit, they are riven.

We are sighing, we are sighing,
　　For the loved ones that have fled;
Those who sojourned in this vineyard,
　　But now are numbered with the dead.

We are thinking, we are thinking,
　　Of that boat upon the tide;
Of the millions it has landed
　　Over on the other side.

We are watching, we are watching,
　　Watching as they pass along,
O'er this rough and winding way,
　　Until they join that shining throng.

We are drawing, we are drawing,
　　Drawing nigh the golden walls,
Where within the portals wide,
　　The everlasting sunshine falls.

Our Thoughts.

Our days are short, our years are few,
    Our path is steep and rough and wide,
But there's a home that's free from toil;
    It lies across that rolling tide

Some are cut down in early morn,
    And borne across those waters deep,
To join the great eternal throng,
    Where angels do their vigils keep.

Some fall at noon when life is sweet;
    The message is to all, "prepare,
Obey the law that is divine,
    Then you shall gain a home up there."

Through sun and storm some day till eve
   They see the changes mortals brave;—
The infant in its cradle rests:
   Toil comes at noon; at night, the grave.

But so it is, thus some one said,—
   Lo! Jacob cried in days of old,
"My years are few, and evil, too,
   But now I'm called into the fold."

Burning of Richmond Theatre.

[A melancholy event in the history of Richmond was the burning of the Theatre, on the night of Dec. 26, 1811, by which the Governor of the state and many others perished in the flames.]

'TWAS on that well-remembered night,
　　When all were heard to say,
　"The night is long, the troupe's in town,
　　We'll go and see the play."

And so they gathered from the town—
　　Six hundred souls or more—
To watch the play upon the stage,
　　As they had done before.

Talent and beauty were gathered there,—
And Virginia's Governor, too,—

Not thinking that death would claim the best
  Ere they saw the actors through.

The play began; all mindswere fixed
  So intently on the scene,
That naught but death could throw a veil
  Their minds and the stage between.

The scenery caught from a chandelier,
  Then the drapery caught on high,
And blazed throughout that stricken crowd
  Like lightning in the sky.

The strong and great trod down the weak—
  Nor knew that they were there;—
Unmindful of their piercing shrieks
  That filled the red-hot air.

In vain they plead for help to come;
  Their shrieks grew loud at every breath;
And then the angry flames replied,
  "My work is sure and certain death!"

The frightful sound of bursting flames,
  The writhing groans of deep despair;
They all arose from that solemn spot,
  And floated off on the midnight air.

When men were leaping to the ground,
  There rose a piercing cry, "where can our
    Governor be?"
And but the roaring flames replied,
  "I've sealed his destiny!"

When that reaper had done his work,
  And death had claimed his own,
Among the names that filled that list,
  Was Virginia's honored son.

She Died With the Old Year.

HE snow was falling thick and fast,
   O'er woodland, town and city, too;—
The piercing blast went sweeping by
   And filled the streets and alleys through.
The earth was robed in spotless white;—
   The merry sleigh-bells seemed to say,
"Improve your time, both old and young,
   For lo! the old year dies to-night!"

The street lamps lit the passers by,
   Their welcome rays shone forth on all—
The old, the young, the rich, the poor—
   On marble fronts and cottage wall.
Yes, the dear old year was dying,
   Its latest hours were waning fast;

When they heard the chime at midnight
    They'd speak of it as of the past.

Lo! what was that year unveiling?
    Was it naught but mirth and gold?
Happy children's ringing laughter,
    Gayest robes of worth untold!
Mines of gold and costly mansions,
    Decked with lace and rarest art,
Where no sighing dared to enter,
    Where festive pleasures filled the heart.

Ah, no; among that crowd
    That passed the street-lamps' flickering
        light,
Went a child with a tattered robe,
    And a heart that sickened at the sight.
Of all things rare that tempt the eye—
    For he thought of the cold and dismal
        room,
And the pallet of straw where his mother
    lie.

He knew she had striven with anguish,
    Her heart was crushed with despair;

Her form, so slender, was yielding
   To its mountain of sorrow and care.

The biting storm that chilled his frame,
   The fleecy snow that filled the air,
They did not check his onward course,
   Nor drive his thoughts from that room so
      bare.
For well he knew that want was feeding
   Upon her vital part;
That strengthened hope and every nerve,
   And that lone and anxious heart.

He'll brave the cold and driving storm,
   And try what love will do
To win his father from the haunts of vice
   To share their grief and woe.
Hungry and weary on he strode,
   Unmindful of the street-lamps' light,
Until he reached that vile abode
   Where virtue sickens at the sight.

He grasped his father's nervous hand,
   And saw his sunken, blood-shot eye,

Then begged him come, for mother's sake,
  With bread ere she should die.
He went with a slow and staggering tread
  By the street-lamps' flickering light;
As reeling, he opened a well-known door
  And said: "Will you trust me for bread
    to-night?"

Again through the dimly lighted streets
  That father went trudging home,
As the night winds howled their dismal
    sounds
  O'er stately trees and towering dome.

When they reached that dismal room,
  Where no brilliant light was streaming,
There that famished mother lay:
  She was not dead, nor sweetly dreaming.
But waiting, waiting, wearily waiting,
  While the moments passed away,
Shivering by the dying embers,
  As on her couch of straw she lay.

As she gazed on the dying embers,
　　She thought of her childhood's happy
　　　　home;
Where, beneath the stately trees,
　　She loved each day to roam.
Of the dear old wall by the garden walk
　　That with ivy was o'er grown,
The constant sound of the dear old rill,
　　With its pure white crested foam.

And the odor of the roses,
　　And the bed of violets rare,
That sent their sweetest fragrance
　　Through all the summer air.
Just twenty years had come and gone
　　Since she vowed to love but one;
And then he was a noble man—
　　A generous, kind and loving son

But woe unto the maddening drink
　　That wildly racks the brain;
'Twill crush the mother's fondest hope,
　　And bind her with a chain!

That father reeled and clasped her hand,
  Her face was deathly pale and fair,
But on his brow was remorse and shame,
  And in that vague unmeaning stare.
Something had reached his callous heart,
  And its hardened fountains stirred;
He tried to speak, but on his tongue
  Faltered and died each word.

Then burning tears, like drops of rain,
  Rolled down that father's face,
Where rum and the lowest haunts of vice
  Had scathed and left their trace.
Her vital part was hunger-bitten;
  That father knew her end was near.
Just as the midnight chime pealed forth,
  That mother died with the old, old year!

The Stolen Child.

H! take me to my home once more,
    To friends and kindred, take me back;
I long to leave these savage haunts,
    My heart grows faint upon the track.

You took me from my mother's arms,—
    Those arms would gladly clasp me now;
I feel the kiss she gave me last,
    The hand that pressed my childish brow.

Long have I been within your tribe,
    And marched o'er Indian trails so long;
I hate the bow and scalping-knife,—
    I hate the savage warrior's song!

My soul 'twas formed for nobler deeds;
  O'er hills and plains I cannot roam;
Oh, grant me but my only wish,
  That is, to see my native home!

'Tis there my brothers are as free
  As soars aloft the eagle's wing;
'Tis there they wait and watch for me,—
  My chair is vacant when they sing.

Now say that you will set me free!
   I'd rather die than linger here!
In dreams I hear my mother's voice;
   In dreams I see the falling tear.

'Tis done, 'tis past, I'm free once more;
   My native land I'll soon behold.
That spot is dearer now to me
   Than rarest gems all decked with gold.

When We Are Old.

—·∘◦◦⊰⊱◦◦∘·—

ERE we're aware—ah! yes, how soon!—
    Will life's bright morning change to
                noon;—
And noon's broad and dazzling light
Put on its sombre robes of night,
And like a story often told,
Will seem our life—when we are old.

To us, when old, this tempting earth
Will lose its rarest charms of mirth;—
All things will have an under-tone
Of quiet—not by right their own;
The summer flowers will still unfold
Their fragrance sweet—when we are old.

When we are old, we will not care,
To paint our face and dye our hair;
'Twill be no great desire then,
In gay and costly robes to shine,
Earthly fame and glittering gold,
Will lose their charms—when we are old.

When we are old, come when that will,
We'll cling to earth a little still;
We'll think it hard that we so soon
Have run the race that others run;
We'll sigh, and think that death is bold
To take us off when we are old.

When we are old, we then shall know
What 'tis to sojourn here below;
We'll know who were our friends indeed,
For, truth, such friends, are friends in need;
If they were sometimes warm, then cold,
They'll be the same when we are old.

When we are old, we all will be
Like tendrils clinging to a tree,
Our hands that toil from sun to sun,

Will need a staff to lean upon;
Our feet, so reckless, quick, and bold,
Will move so slow when we are old.

When we are old—those words now seem
Like the rehearsal of a dream—
We picture, as in prophetic rhyme,
That far-off spot on the shore of time—
That spot so distant, it seems quite bold;
Even to say when we are old.

When we are old—perhaps ere then,
We shall be borne from the haunts of men;
For lo! our dwelling may be found
Beneath the cold and silent ground;
Our name perchance may be enrolled
Among the dead—ere we are old.

Ere we are old,—that time is now,—
For youth and noon are on our brow.
Let not the moments idly fall—
Life has a thousand charms for all,
And some will always an influence hold
Within our minds—when we are old.

Ere we are old, let each one give
Their hours in learning how to live,
Then we shall meet with ready heart,
At noon, the message come depart;
Or feel our latest days consoled,
By God's great love—when we are old.

Wild Cat Money in the 50s

Wild Cat Money in the '50s.

———✦———

THEY had a peculiar kind of money in the '50s—in those good old days ! They called it by pet and elegant names, such as "White Dog," "Blue Pup," and "Wild Cat."

When a man had worked hard for a month and received his wages, he didn't know how much he was worth.

He would go home and his wife would say, "Supper is ready." "Wait a little," he would reply, "until I see how much money I have." Then he would begin sorting it out in three piles. He remembered the "White Dog" had forty-seven cents discount; "Blue Pup" thirty-six cents discount; "Wild

Cat" seventy-three cents discount. His wife would call him again to supper, but he was not ready. He would commence figuring out discounts, while his wife, impatiently waiting, would say, "Why don't you come to supper!"

The supper would get cold, and the tired and brain-worn father had no appetite to eat; but after the discount was counted out, and he knew the worst, and had to abide by it, with depressed feeling he took his accustomed place at the table and tried to make himself agreeable, knowing his wife and children were not to blame for the financial trouble that was coursing through his brain.

He ate a light meal, thinking all the while, discount, discount, discount. After supper he had no inclination to read, but repaired to a corner absorbed in deep thought, thinking if this state of things continued much longer he would as soon see a general conflagration sweep our land to destruction.

With such thoughts coursing through his brain he was far from being attractive. His downcast looks made his children shy; they did not care to climb upon his knee as they were wont to do, but tried to get out of his sight. He retired earlier than usual and soon fell into a restless sleep, and his wife would hear him muttering, as he rolled uneasily from side to side, "Discount," "Discount," "Blue Pup," "White Dog," "Wild Cat," "Forty-seven Cents," "Thirty-nine Cents" and "Seventy-three Cents." "Oh, dear Jane, such a government to pay a man in rags for hard labor faithfully performed! It is too much for flesh and blood to bear!" His wife tries to awaken him from his troubled sleep, but he only mutters, "discount," "discount."

He awakes in the morning with a headache; his wife doesn't know whether to be affectionate or not, but feels deeply the trouble that is weighing her husband down. He partakes of his breakfast with as little

relish as he ate his supper, and then goes
forth to earn some more "discount."

This is a faithful picture of many a home
in "Wild Cat Money Days." How different
the picture is now. A man gets his money
and has nothing to do but to turn over the
corners of the bills to see if there is the
right amount, roll it up and put it into his
pocket, knowing he has been paid for honest labor in honest money—money that has
no pet names and no discount.

Boys, don't Run Away from Home.

———◦◦◦°°°◦◦◦———

HROUGH cities, towns and villages,
   No matter where we roam;
Through gorgeous frescoed palaces,
   There's not a spot like home.

We bid farewell to home and friends,
   To sail across the briny foam,
To view the land by Israel trod,
   But our hearts will yearn for home.

The youthful lad who spurns control,
   And with strangers loves to roam,
Will stop and think in his reckless course,
   Of the loving ones at home.

Now, boys, no matter what's your lot,
   For trials you have some;
Don't think you'll top the stair of fame,
   By running away from home.

In choosing a guide, take my advice:—
   Don't counsel with those who roam,
And cause your mother dear to weep,
   By running away from home.

She's toiled from morn till dewy eve,
   Her life is naught but care,
Till on her brow the trace is left,
   And in her silvered hair.

The rosy tint has left her cheek,
   She's cared for you so long;
So while you're a boy and needing care,
   Don't run away from home.

Take my advice: her counsel heed,
   And ever strive to give her rest;
Then your conscience will not smite,
   When the clay falls on her breast.

You cannot find in a time of need,
  No matter where you roam,
A friend so true, and a spot so dear,
  As a mother, and a home.

So when the tempter lures you on,
  And dazzling lights have shone,
Just ask your mother if 'tis best
  To run away from home.

Childhood's Days.

THE dearest scenes that swell the heart,
  Are the happy days of childhood;
  When we were free as the timid fawn
    That roams through glen and wild-wood;
    Those days are passed and gone.

We had no cares to oppress the mind,
Nor a heart cast down by sorrow.
Each day flew past like a lovely dream,
Unmindful of the morrow;—
  Those happy days of childhood.

O! that word brings scenes so sweet!
That family board where all would meet

On memory's tablet each face appears,
That formed the household wreath for years;
 That wreath is torn apart.

The sweet, sweet years of a happy child,
Roaming among the wood-land wild;
Or whiling away the sultry hours
In cottage, hall, or shady bowers;
 Those hours are past and gone.

Or listening to the stories told,
Around the hearth-stone, rude and old;
When the father's work was done,
And the merry twilight hour had come;—
 That hour will come no more.

Or we'd sit on our father's knee,
And watch his thoughtful brow,
With our childish hands in his soft, brown
 hair;—
Those locks are silvery now;—
 Those locks, so fair, are gone.

The damask rose, and wild-briar sweet,
That with fragrance filled the air,
And the busy bee culled all day long
From the apple blossoms rare.
    Oh! those apple trees!

We see a change, a noted change,
For other children leave their plays
And bound away to Grandpa's knee
To hear rich tales of childhood's days--
    Those days when we were young.

Our childhood days, so fair and bright,
They chase away the clouds of night.
If care and trials be our lot,
We'll look on them as one bright spot,
    Where care and sorrow cometh not.

Oh, those dear, those sacred scenes;
Like a mountain peak they rise;
We long to view those scenes once more
That we once viewed with childish eyes;
    Those scenes we'll view no more.

Our cherished school-days—Oh! how sweet
Those words, they bring the falling tear.
As death has claimed some of the best,
Our school-mates dear for many a year.
   Lo! now they sweetly rest.

The name of childhood—Oh how sweet!
It cheers the prisoner in his cell.
That word, so dear, points out a path
And binds him with a magic spell—
   Unto the days of childhood.

All are stronger, nobler, wiser,
Under life's mature reign,
But we feel that pleasures sweet
Were showered around our childish feet—
   And never will return again.

Childhood's days—how quick they vanish;
And we sigh for them in vain.
They surround us, we behold them every-
   where,
As the childish laughter rings through the
   balmy air;—
   But they'll never come again.

Cyclone

SEE! the sky is hid from view!
 The blackened clouds are gathering
  now!
Shut the windows! close the doors!
 The farmer leaves his work and plow!

It's hurry and bustle, here and there,
 To care for all about;
For the frightful storm appears to say,
 "My path I have marked out!"

The deep-voiced thunders peal afar,
 As if to rend the sky,
And add to the gloom of the coming storm,
 Now watched by every eye.

Cyclone.

The cloudy pillars roll on high,
  As if they longed to say,
"I'm stronger than the flood and fire!
  No mortals can me stay!"

With inky blackness and rumbling sound,
  The storm king wends his way,
Like troops engaged in deadly strife,
  To see who'll win the day.

It sweeps the ground, then soars on high,
  And bears its reapings through the air;
While all along the path it chose,
  Ascends the wail of sore despair!

With furious speed it rolls along;
  Clouds dashing, then clashing,
Downward, then upward,
  Collecting, then scattering
    Its wrecks through the air.

The groans of the strong, and shrieks of the
    frantic!

Blackness, despair, desolation and death,
Are the scenes that are witnessed
When earth has been visited by the
   Cyclone's breath.

Admonition.

———◦◦◦⊛◦◦◦———

N view of all the suffering and war that American fathers, mothers, sons and daughters have been called upon to endure, allow me to give you a word of advice, knowing that our sons will soon be called upon to occupy seats in our executive, legislative and judicial departments; knowing the time is fast approaching when they will be called upon to make the laws that govern this great and powerful nation; we ought to teach them to live upright and honorable lives; teach them that wisdom is better than rubies, and a good name is rather to be chosen than great riches. If they are fortunate enough to accumulate any wealth, teach them not to become oppressors. If they happen to wear the badge of office, to not be a political knave.

A rich man who has been an oppressor—his name will fade away before the death-sweat comes upon his brow; and when he dies, there is a wreath of glory about him. He can look around and see that it is a palace in which he is breathing his last. He has millions which he can call his own. He will raise his glassy eye and look out of his window once more, and reflect that all within and far beyond the range of his vision belongs to him. He thinks how his name has rung through the land;—yes, through the world! Millions who have never seen his face, are familiar with his fame.

He is dying, but it is not a vulgar death. There is no proverty there. He is dying, but he thinks the pagentry that will attend his funeral is itself worth dying for. He is dying, but he thinks his name will never die; he thinks that will live through the

vicissitudes of many generations. He thinks
the worm that will devour his body can not
mar the glory of that name. He can see it
emblazoned on every paper throughout the
world. But the name of an oppressor will
fade and sink into obscurity.

Many have been left to struggle with
poverty, unassisted and unbefriended, because oppressors ruled. Many have been
deprived of their natural rights, because
oppressors were exhalted to power.

An oppressor, with all the means of use-
fullness at his command, which this world
can furnish, lives for purposses of mere sel-
fish gratification; and when he dies is never
missed—except in the sense you miss an
oppressive burden. No one mourns his
death, except his near relatives—and no
doubt part of those are over-joyed to hear
that the oppressor is gone. The community
in which he lived will call it an act of Providence in removing such an one, and will be
ready to place the last sod above his mortal

remains. Nothing exhalts the character more than the habitual exercise of a benevolent spirit: a man, whom money has placed in a condition far above that of any other individual in the community in which he has lived, moving about among his inferiors with affibility and kindness, apparently forgetful of his wealth and his honors. Ready to speak a word of consolation, or make an offering of charity, wherever it is needed. Benevolent institutions reckon on him as a benefactor. Destitute widows are made to rejoice amidst their sorrow because of his kindness; and many an orphan child would, without any prompting, speak forth his praise. There will be an attraction in his look and manner that will make the little child eager to climb upon his knee to do him honor. You will see him moving about with as little parade as one of his tenants. When such an one dies the tidings of his death will bring mourning to all hearts. Every one who has become familiar with his name will mourn his departure; mourn the loss of one who has been so gentle and kind; one with such a warm and generous heart and dignified manners; one who could accommodate himself to all the different kinds of society.

To the fathers and mothers who navigated that stormy sea twenty years ago, if you would avoid another such a tempestuous voyage, teach your children to support the constitution and obey the laws of our nation. Teach them that they may be inspired with the same feelings which inspired Webster when he made that memorable speech on liberty and disunion. Allow me to quote a portion of it for the benefit of those who may not be familiar with it:

"Mr. President: I shall enter on no encomium upon Massachusetts; she needs none. There she is,—behold her and judge for yourself. There is her history,—the world knows it by heart. The past, at least, is secure. There is Boston, and Concord, and

Lexington, and Bunker Hill; and there they will remain forever. The bones of her sons, fallen in the great struggle for independence, now lie mingled with the soil of every state from New England to Georgia; and there they will lie forever. And, sir, where American liberty raised its first voice, and where its youth was nurtured and sustained, there it still lives in the strength of its manhood, and full of its original spirit! If discord and disunion shall wound it; if party strife and blind ambition shall hawk at and tear it; if folly and madness, if uneasiness, under salutary and necessary restraint, shall succeed to separate it from that union, by which alone is existence made sure, it will stand in the end by the side of that cradle in which its infancy was rocked; it will stretch forth its arm with whatever of vigor it may still retain over the friends who gathered round it, and it will fall at last, if fall it must, amidst the proudest monuments of its own glory, and on the very spot of its origin. * *

"I profess, sir, in my career hitherto to have kept steadily in view the prosperity and honor of the whole country, and the preservation of our Federal union. It is to that union we owe safety at home, and our consideration and dignity abroad. It is to that union that we are chiefly indebted for whatever makes us most proud of our country. That union we reached only by the discipline of our virtues in the severe school of adversity. It had its origin in the necessities of disordered finance, prostrate commerce, and ruined credit. Under its benign influences these great interests immediately awoke as from the dead, and sprang forth with newness of life. Every year of its duration has teemed with fresh proofs of its utility and its blessings; and although our territory has stretched out wider and wider, and our population spread further and further, they have not outrun its protection, or its benefits. It has been to us all a copious fountain of national, social and personal happiness. I have not allowed myself, sir, to look beyond the union to see what might lie hidden in the dark recess behind. I have not coolly weighed the chances of preserving liberty when the bonds that unite us together shall be broken asunder. I have not accustomed myself to hang over the precipice of disunion to see whether, with my short sight, I can fathom the depth of the abyss below; nor could I regard him as a safe counselor in the affairs of this government, whose thoughts should be mainly bent on considering, not how the Union should be best preserved, but how tolerable might be the condition of the people when it shall be broken up and destroyed. While the Union lasts we have high, exciting, gratifying prospects spread out before us, and our children. Beyond that I seek not to penetrate the veil. God grant that, in my day, at least, that curtain may not rise! God grant that on my vision never may be opened what lies behind! When my eyes shall be turned to

behold, for the last time, the sun in heaven,
may I not see it shining on the broken and
dishonored fragments of a once glorious
Union; on States dissevered, discordant,
belligerent; on a land rent with civil feuds,
or drenched, it may be, in fraternal blood!
Let their last feeble and lingering glance
rather behold the gorgeous ensign of the republic, now known and honored throughout
the earth, still full high advanced, its arms
and trophies, streaming in their original lus-
tre, not a stripe erased or polluted, nor a
single star obscured,—bearing for its motto
no such miserable interrogatory as 'What is
all this worth?' nor those other words of de-
lusion and folly, 'Liberty first, and union af-
terward!' but everywhere, spread all over in
characters of living light, blazing on all its
ample folds, as they float over the sea and
over the land, and in every wind under the
whole heavens, that other sentiment, dear to
every true American heart, 'Liberty and Union, now and forever, one and inseperable!'"

Yes, teach them to love liberty and despise oppression and treason, trample that combined monster in the dust before it has charmed them and entwined them within its folds so it can sting the vital part as it once stung this nation.

We hear people talking a great deal of late about corruption. What and where is corruption? You may be robbed of your pocket-book and all of its contents, but what is that in comparison to being confronted by a man, your neighbor, with a loaded revolver which he will thrust into your face and blow your brains out because you have differed from him politically some time previous. That is the kind of corruption we saw for years, and certainly no patriotic son desires to have such corruption forced upon us again. Ask that long list of fathers, mothers, sons and daughters who are mourning the loss of loved ones, who were torn from their household by a bloodthirsty rebellion,—ask them concerning cor-

ruption; ask that long list of ex-Union soldiers, who are to-day dying as it were by
inches from wounds inflicted upon the battle-
field and from diseases contracted while in
camp and prison-pens,—ask them about corruption; ask the millions of Africa's sons,
who groaned under the galling chains of
their oppressors,—ask them concerning corruption. Combine the lists and ask them
all, and they will tell you that all the combined corruptions of this planet are nothing
in comparison with the corruption that issues
from the wound of treason. That is a deadly
poison. They will tell you that the air which
surrounds the head of that monster is so
contaminated with the germs of death that
it will slay its tens of thousands without the
right preventative in time. Those who are
crying corruption, before they cry it any
more they had better transform their swords
into plow-shares and their gun-barrels into
railroad iron, so there will be neither wars
nor rumors of wars, and neighbor cease to

lift up his hand against neighbor, and have cruelty and persecution stop, and have the south, as well as the north, blossom as the rose.

To those who stood in the ranks of the Republican party and saw the national treasury emptied in a time of peace—no, I won't say peace, for there was no peace— when there was shooting, stabbing, hanging, taring and feathering, and hounding from place to place; you who stood in the ranks of the Republican party and saw our nation gagged and dragged to the very brink of ruin, you saw that powerful flood ready any moment to break through and engulf us all in the black and dismal waters of anarchy, slavery and despair; you saw the Republican party, thus bound down, take control of this government with one-half of the continent banded against it, and an army ready for battle; you saw the Republican party snap the chain that bound them, arm and equip two millions of men to maintain our national integrity; arm and equip brother to fight brother, because the house was divided; one wanted an aristocracy and crush American manufactories and build monopolies in old England; the other party wanted what the old flag waved—peace, prosperity, civilization, progress, and all kinds of internal improvements. It assures protection to life, property, public credit, and the payment of the debt of the government, state, county, or municipality. So far as it has control, it fosters the production of the field and farm, and of the manufactories. It encourages the general education of the poor as well as the rich. It is a party of progress and of liberality toward its opponents; it encourages the poor to strive to better their condition; the ignorant to educate their children, to enable them to compete successfully with their more fortunate associates; and, in fine, it secures an entire equality, before the law, of every citizen—every one has the opportunity to make himself all he is capable of,

The Republican party is a party of principle; the same principles prevailing wherever it has a foothold. The Republican party has done all that has been done for the advancement of civilization and the up-building of American industries. The Republican party is breaking the way for future ages. Those coming after us will look across the billows of that stormy sea that you have navigated and will see high up the peak the pennon of the Republican party, looking at the light-house, which the Republican party has been building on the path of time. Posterity will see eternal sunshine settle on their heads. The flag of the Republican party, more worthy than any other ever borne in human hands, is radiant and resplendant with illustrious achievements. You saw the Republican party born anew. In the throes of a moral and military earthquake. You saw it organize the armies, the fleets, and finances, which fought successfully the most gigantic war in history. You saw it liberate

.our millions of slaves. You saw it establish
an absolute free republic. You saw it re-
generate the national constitution. You saw
it build its house upon a rock, and the floods
came, and the rains descended, and the winds
blew and beat upon it, and it fell not. You
saw the Republican party do all these things.
You saw it rescue from destruction a nation-
ality incomparably the greatest the world
has ever seen, and having done all these
things you saw that party stand; therefore
you ought not to be for it a little but a great
deal. You sat by its cradle, you toiled in
its ranks at noon, and now by any act of
yours, no matter whether you have been
disappointed or not, would you hand this
Government over into the hands of those
who tried by every means that men could
devise to crush that bright and shining star?
tried to trample out that glorious tree of
American liberty, whose roots were watered
by the blood of the most patriotic sons the
world ever new, in more than twenty battles

during the Revolution, and has been nurtured by unflinching sons possessed with
unalloyed and pure devotion to the Union?
If you have any love for your country, any
feelings for your sons or for the generations
to follow, I ask, will you, by any wrangling,
disappointment, or any act, follow its hearse?

Green Longmans, Digby Collins

The Horse-Trainer's and Sportsman's Guide
with additional condiserations on the duties of grooms, on purchasing blood stock, and on veterinary examination

ISBN/EAN: 9783337392482

Printed in Europe, USA, Canada, Australia, Japan

Cover: Foto ©Andreas Hilbeck / pixelio.de

More available books at **www.hansebooks.com**

THE

HORSE - TRAINER'S AND

SPORTSMAN'S GUIDE;

WITH ADDITIONAL CONSIDERATIONS

ON THE DUTIES OF GROOMS, ON PURCHASING BLOOD STOCK,

AND ON VETERINARY EXAMINATION.

BY   DIGBY   COLLINS.

.

LONDON:

LONGMANS,   GREEN,   AND   CO.

1865.